Lord, Save Me From Myself

SECOND EDITION

OLIVIA SHAW-REEL

Soul Cry Saga book covers designed by Paris Reel of Reel Designs. Heart vector by tartila, obtained at freepik.com.

ISBN: 978-1-7360500-6-4

A Message from the Author

This book contains triggering situations and mentions of abuse, suicide, and violence.

Acknowledgments

To everyone responsible for the woman I am:

My GOD – Father, may You be glorified with every word I write and every day that I live for You.

My MUSE – Baby, I appreciate you for the book covers and those fun yet intense moments of bouncing off ideas to you.

My TRIBE – I love and thank you for the unending encouragement.

My SUPPORTERS – You make writing so worthwhile!

LOVE ALWAYS,
OSR

Prologue

Jalen Owens

Church was not the place for my unclean and inappropriate thoughts, but I was helpless to stop the fantasy running through my mind.

"Lord, we praise You! Lord, we love and honor You! Thank You for Your visitation this morning," the worship leader cried out.

She had her eyes closed and a hand was lifted in worship. The royal blue and silver glitter nail polish combination on her fingernails could have been distracting, if it weren't for the soulful reverence that flowed from her lips. The microphone that she sang into was positioned perfectly in front of her heart-shaped mouth. I gazed at the microphone stand. It, too, was positioned just right before her five-foot frame.

I was not sure of her name, but I knew that I wanted to get to know her better. My eyes fell to the outfit she wore. The flowy dress hung loosely from her body, but I could tell she was a petite woman with a few subtle curves. It was appropriate for worship but unsuitable for my thoughts that ran rampant.

As she moved around the stage, my eyes moved with her legs that were captive in fishnet stockings. I licked my lips, imagining how beautiful and perfect she must have looked in just her bare skin. I wondered what kind of underwear she wore. She was probably a matching panty and bra type of woman. I wondered if she was *really* saved, or if she was an undercover freak like me. Was she married?

There was definitely a ring on her left hand. Did I care? Absolutely not.

No one truly knew that I had a problem with lust and sex. No one knew that I was once an award-winning, God-fearing pastor at a mega church. No one realized that I was almost the mayor of my town, up until controversy disrupted my campaign. No one knew that I was in the running to be the presiding bishop over all of the Pentecostal churches in the Midwest region up until my downfall. No one knew I once had the best wife and companion a man could ever pray for and had messed it up time and time again by slapping her around, verbally abusing her, and doing everything else under the sun. I had divorced her and drifted from God, thinking I could do things on my own, but that was furthest from the truth. I had stolen money from my church; I had slept with the same women I counseled, and I had taken away the trust of my members.

The church as I knew it crumbled—not physically, but spiritually. With God no longer in the equation, I thought that I could do what I wanted, when I wanted, and how I wanted. Boy, was I wrong. Now, as I sat in a completely different city, in the third row of a totally different church, I realized that I still had not confronted the *real* problem that had destroyed my life and everything in it. I was still very much addicted. Temptation called me everywhere I went, and I answered to it even after all the turmoil it had brought to my life.

The young lady singing her heart out helped none as I stood up and made my way towards the side of the semi-large church. I was going to catch her as she came down so that I could greet her. This was my fourth time at this church's Tuesday service, and I was beginning to like everything about the establishment. This was a "come as you are" church, so this was ideal for my situation. I was not perfect—I loved God, but I did not allow that same God to fully deliver me from my shortcomings and strongholds. I was still a man with lust in my heart, and at this point, the sickness couldn't be stopped.

The praise and worship team ended their 30-minute set and then the assistant pastor stepped onto the pulpit to greet members and visitors. I pressed my back to the wall as the choir walked past, heading to their seats throughout the church. As the worshipper passed by, who had blessed my soul in more ways than one, I grabbed her arm and nodded for her to follow me outside.

"Service is starting," she told me as if I did not already know.

"I won't be long. What's your name?" I asked, still holding onto her arm.

She looked uncomfortable and unsure. I was still a new face around the church, so she probably assumed I was some crazy guy dropping in.

"Why? I'm not interested."

"You have to be interested to give me your name? Wow. That's not right at all. I just wanted to compliment your voice. You really touched my spirit this morning," I spoke truthfully, softening my tone. I finally let go of her arm and looked around. "I'm new to town and I've been actively searching for a church home. Today's worship reeled me in. I'm seriously thinking about joining."

"That's awesome, and I apologize if I came off rude. It's just that…" She pointed backward towards the church. "…I didn't want my dad looking for me and worrying. Plus, I have to lead the sermonic song before Pastor gets up, so I wanted to grab a cough drop really quick and rest my voice. I'm happy God led you here though."

"Yeah, me too," I agreed, tugging at my neatly trimmed goatee and then extending my hand. "So, may I please have your name? I'm Jalen."

"I'm Daley," she introduced herself finally, blushing as I took the back of her hand and kissed it. She immediately tucked her hand against her side shyly. "Where did you fellowship before?"

I ignored her question. "Are you married or seeing anyone, Daley? You're very beautiful."

"*Married*? I'm ONLY seventeen!" she exclaimed, giggling and then heading back towards the entryway. "We must get back inside. Dad will be looking for…"

My heart dropped at how juvenile she was. The ring on her finger must have been some sort of purity or promise ring. As she rambled on about her dad coming to look for her, I shook my head free of any unclean thoughts and figured I would try my luck with some other woman at another time. I felt like a complete idiot and just needed to drown myself in the Word of God to feel somewhat decent again. But I never got my chance.

As I followed her back into the church, I was bum-rushed by a group of men all wearing black and who looked like they were not up for games or conversation. Daley ran off fearfully, seeming to recognize the man at the forefront of the security guards. They pulled me outside and crossed their arms.

"Was all that necessary?" I shouted, dusting my suit jacket off and adjusting my clothes coolly. "What's the problem?"

The wind was knocked out of me and I could feel my nose nearly break as a fist came my way, connecting with my face. I fell to the ground, groaning, and tried to look up at who had taken the cheap shot. It had to have been the salt and pepper-haired man with the double-breasted suit on. He looked the angriest of the group and sort of favored Daley.

"The problem is PUNKS like you coming into the church and preying on little girls! That's my daughter whose hand you were kissing! I know about you. I've read about your ways and schemes. You're that pathetic pastor who was kicked out of his own church a few years back. I hope you don't think you're going to come in here and stir up some mess?"

I guess I was not as unknown as I thought. Trouble continued to follow me, and I had no one to blame but myself. I guess that was my fault for always running behind a pretty face and gorgeous body. I should have known Daley was too young for me. I was in my early 40s and must have looked like a pedophile flirting with her. I had daughters practically her age, so I understood his anger.

"If you know what's good for you, you'll never show your face around here again. Otherwise, I'll help you meet Jesus *reeeeal* quick," the man continued, patting his side where an obvious firearm was tucked. I could see the print of the handgun, even with tears in my eyes.

"I'm sorry," I said lowly. "I didn't know she was underage, man."

There was nothing more to be said. I gathered my things and held a hand over my bloody nose as I headed to the car. The security guards watched me as I pulled out of the parking lot like a racecar driver, never to be seen again.

Needless to say, I would *not* be joining that church today.

Chapter One

"*Sssss*," I hissed as I stared in the rearview mirror at my swollen, slightly disfigured nose and touched the tip of it. The punch was a devastating blow. The man had fractured my nose, but thankfully, no surgery was needed. After an emergency room visit and a few cold compresses and medication, I was finally on my way back home with a bloodstained suit and bloodstained shoes. If I wanted, I could press charges, but ultimately, I was wrong for coming at his daughter the way I did. After all, if it were my beautiful *underage* baby girls, I would have been irate too.

Speaking of my daughters, Summer and Autumn, I had not seen them in what felt like forever. Since moving to Waukegan, Illinois, it was hard to see them as frequently as I once did. They no longer lived with me since their mother left me for the next man with a nice car, immaculate house, and impressive bank account. I guess that was another punishment for doing God's people wrong. As my mother used to tell me as a young boy, "You reap what you sow."

I pulled into the parking lot of my apartment complex that was nothing like the home I once owned and loved. It was mediocre, and nothing really special to it. Nevertheless, I enjoyed my little secluded spot, and was happy that I was far away from the people of my past. Most of my neighbors were sweet elderly white folks who talked my ear off whenever I went downstairs to get the mail or throw trash away. I greeted one now as I waved and ducked my head, trying to avoid explaining why I had a fractured nose.

Miss Eliza did not take the hint and continued going on and on about the neighbor's barking dog. I nodded, acting as if I was interested as I unlocked my mailbox and retrieved the sales paper and bills that were stacked inside. There was a flyer that was mixed in with my mail, and it caught my eye immediately.

On the front side, my ex-wife was seated at a desk. She wore a bright smile with her head cocked to the side and her petite hands were crossed. It was your typical professional photo, staged in a library. On the desk were several stacked books that were turned towards the camera, entitled *I Survived*. The text on the flyer read:

Book Signing with Author Jamaika Daniels
Free Entry, Refreshments, and Raffles

I checked the date and saw that the book signing was coming up in another two weeks. I hung the flyer on my refrigerator once I escaped Mother Motor Mouth—*I mean*, Miss Eliza. It still tripped me out that Jamaika was no longer mine, and most importantly, that I had allowed her to get away. Yes, I divorced *her*, but in doing that, I still allowed her to move on and marry another man. For more than a decade, she shared my last name, my space, my world, and everything in it but I had taken her for granted. I had lost her forever.

She looked good, and she looked happy— happier than I could have ever made her. Her normally boring, conservative wardrobe and look had undergone a major upgrade. She had lost weight and toned up well, dyed and cut her hair, and her skin was glowing as if there was some sort of filter over the photograph. I could not believe she had written a book. It was something that she always wanted to do but was too insecure to execute.

The title alone intrigued me. *I Survived*. I wondered, was she referring to her suicide attempt? Was she talking about me in the book and telling readers that she survived my wrath, fists, and insults? Either way, I had to find out for myself, and made a mental note to try to come out and support. It was the *least* I could do for all the hell I gave her for most of our marriage.

In the meantime, I needed nourishment. I was an okay cook, but I had a few frozen TV dinners that would satisfy my appetite. I placed a broccoli and chicken fettuccine dinner in the microwave, put it on high for three minutes, and then headed to the bedroom. I could finally change out of my church garments and strip down to boxers, an undershirt, and socks that needed washing after today. I turned on a television show and plopped down on the leather sofa.

Because of my actions, this boring life had become the norm. There were no more lavish cars and expensive shopping trips; there was no longer a spacious house to come home to or tropical vacations to book, and there definitely was not a variety of beautiful women everyday of the week. I just had me, myself, and I.

I woke up in the wee hours of the morning to banging on my door and the muffled sounds of someone yelling. Sighing with instant irritation, I climbed out of bed and looked at the digital clock on the nightstand. It was just past six in the morning, and I worked from home, so there was no reason I should have been up at such an hour. Through the thick blanket of darkness, I looked for a shirt to pull on and successfully avoided stubbing my toe on the corner of the dresser. I remained in my boxers and only adjusted them so that I was at least halfway presentable.

"Who is it?" I growled, becoming more and more agitated the closer I got to the door. The knocks were not as frequent and aggressive, but there was definitely a woman going on and on about God knows what. "Do you realize what TIME it…?"

As I threw open the door, my words died off in my throat. My eyes settled on the yelling woman, who had a milk chocolate complexion, dark eyes, and a curvy body. Her cheeks were slightly flushed as she yelled. She wore skintight jeans, wedge sandals, and a blazer with a thin, off the shoulder top beneath. She could have been classy if it were not for the head full of green, yellow, and pink foam rollers. A sheer bonnet completed the look, causing me to roll my eyes and lean completely against the doorframe.

As much as I wanted to yell in return, I couldn't. "Kyla, are you crazy?" I whispered harshly, "You could have waited until later to stop by. Why are you banging on my door at six in the morning? Have you lost your mind—?"

"Let me in!" she demanded.

"Nah, you're going to have to cool it down a little bit first."

"*JALEN*, let me *IN* before I go *OFF!*" she screamed, pushing past me with her elbow. I caught her arm and shoved her into my apartment, hurriedly closing the door. I could hear my neighbors stirring awake in confusion in the apartments surrounding me and did not want to draw any more unwanted attention. "Get your hands off me!"

"Lower your voice and tell me why you're here? I should slap you for making such a ruckus!" I threatened, balling my fists.

Kyla only glared back at me, challenging me to act on it. She knew I wasn't stupid. She wasn't the average female nor was she ever afraid of my threats. Kyla was someone I had slept with a few months back on four different occasions. Our intimacy was nothing memorable, plus she had a longtime husband, so it was easy for us to break apart and move on like nothing happened. That's why I was confused by her presence.

"Look, I had a hair appointment and stopped here on my way. I don't want to be here any more than you want me here. Let's just make this quick."

"Make *what* quick?" I questioned, scratching myself and cocking my head to the side. I did not have time for beating around the bush and playing guessing games. Either she was going to talk, or I was going to head back to bed.

She shuffled through her oversized purse and then came away with a manila folder. Opening the folder, she shoved a piece of paper in my unexpected hands and then settled her weight to one side of her body. "Well?"

I took a single glance at the paper. It was a printout of some sort. It almost looked like a—

"It's an *ultrasound*," she said with attitude, breaking me from my thoughts.

"Yeah, and it's not mine," I said nonchalantly and spun around in my socks, heading back towards the bedroom.

"Not yours? Besides my husband, you think I'd sleep around with other men?"

"I don't know. Would you?" I smirked and kept my cool. She was trying to trap me, and I wasn't having it. "We used protection every time, Kyla. Stop it."

"Condoms *do* break, Jalen. They're only 99.9 percent effective," she reasoned.

I was silent for a moment, watching her without worry or stress. "Nice try. You can lock up on your way out. I know you still have the key."

"Don't flatter yourself, Jalen. I tossed the key out right along with the good times we shared. How dare you imply I'm lying? This baby is yours and I have the evidence to prove it! I'm two steps ahead of you," she said in a crazed manner and then fished around in her purse for another piece of paper. "This is the timeline between my last period, the last time we had sex, and the time of my conception. Hmmph!"

"Yeah, whatever. Get rid of it," I suggested coldly, not even bothering to look at her timeline. I had absolutely no interest in being a baby's daddy to another woman. "Whether it's mine or not, you don't have to keep it. Let's just let it die just like this relationship."

"Are you serious right now? How could you say something like that?" she cried, looking at me as if I was the scum of the earth. "What kind of man are you? You knew the repercussions of having sex with a married woman!"

"Just like you knew the repercussions of having sex with a man who had no feelings for you. What will your husband say? Isn't that going to get you in even more trouble when he finds out?" I asked but was stunned when her fist connected with my jawline.

This was the second time I had been hit off guard by someone in the last 24 hours, and it did not feel good. This time, however, my reflexes weren't so delayed. I slapped Kyla with the back of my hand and watched as she fell to my hardwood floor. I slapped her once more for good measure, and then tugged on her clothes to pick her up. She shoved my hands away with a gasp and refused my help. Her fingertips found the bruised, puffed-up patch of skin that I had inflicted. Her lip was busted and there were fresh tears brimming her eyes.

"*Jalen*," she whispered, shocked and hurt by my actions. "How could you?"

I blinked a few times and forced myself to calm down. She was right. How could I? I realized what I had done, and instantly felt the guilt and shame. "I—I'm sorry! I didn't mean to hit you."

"I guess it *was* true, and all those people weren't lying. You really *are* a woman beater," she accused, struggling to stand and get as far away from me as possible. "You'll be hearing from my lawyer…and my husband!"

She rushed out so suddenly that I could not stop her or apologize to her again. I closed and locked the door behind her, slid down the back of it, and then buried my face in my hands. I was emotional but I refused to cry. I just could not seem to stay out of trouble. Whether it was legal matters, financial setbacks, church discrepancies, or women issues, I was in a world of hurt. I should have never lain down with that woman for a few moments of pleasure. Now I had a 'baby' on the way, two daughters I already could not see, and Lord knows whom else I had gotten pregnant with my promiscuous ways.

Lord, what have I gotten myself into?

Eventually I picked myself up, took a hot shower, and went on about my day. I made sure to put on a bandage that covered up my still swollen and black and blue face. I'm sure I looked ridiculous, but I needed to run to the store to pick up a few toiletries before work began.

I was an at-home marketing director for one of the largest health care companies in the Midwest, and I loved it. The pay was decent, my schedule and flexibility were ideal, and it all took place from the comforts of my home. Plus, my boss was one of my closest friends and had given me the job when I lost my job as senior pastor.

It was still pretty early—just past eight o'clock, so there weren't many people out and about. I headed down the aisle where the deodorant and body washes were. I chose my normal brand name products, tossing them in my shopping basket. I threw a box of Q-tips in as well, and a few rolls of tissue. As I reached for a replacement blade for my razor, my hand collided with another hand, causing a few of the blades to fall from the shelf.

"Oh, I'm sorry." I apologized, bending down to pick up the items I had dropped. Out of my peripheral, I saw a pair of the smoothest, most gorgeous legs I had ever seen. They were without any blemishes, fine hairs, or scars. They belonged to a woman, whom I could only imagine was just as beautiful. I placed the blades back on the shelf and stood to my complete height. "How are you this morning?"

I got a good look at the woman and was not disappointed. She stood at my eye level, which I attributed to her high heels. But without them, I figured she was still around 5'9," give or take an inch. She was the shade of creamy chocolate, with long limbs and a long neck, but her features were *jaw dropping*. She looked like a famous model you would see gracing the covers of magazines, minus the anorexia. She was a healthy size eight or ten. Her dark brown hair was bone-straight and hung just past her shoulder blades. Her dark eyes were accented with a pair of leopard-print eyeglasses. She had to be from some exotic island. American women did not look like this.

"I'm very well. *Tired*," she chuckled, motioning towards the cup of coffee she held in her available hand. She also toted a blue shopping basket with similar items as mine inside. "How are you, love?"

I was amused by the pet name she had already given me. Sure enough, she had a bit of an accent. "I'm alright. Not looking forward to the weather cooling down."

"I know, right? Back in Barbados, we didn't have this kind of weather. I still barely have the right clothes since I moved."

She was confirming all of my assumptions without me asking. I returned her smile and allowed her to walk in front of me as we headed to the checkout.

"Barbados, huh? I've never been, but it sounds and looks beautiful."

"It is. I miss home a lot, but this is my new life," she sighed with a shrug. There was a hint of sadness in her voice. "I like it here so far."

"I'm glad you're liking things so far. Do you have any family here at least?"

Unsurely, she looked around and then shook her head. "It's just me. I've visited America many times, and even lived in New York for three years, but nothing beats the good ole island."

"So, how did you end up in Waukegan of *all* places?"

"*Loooong* story," she stressed. "Very, very long story."

The cashier began ringing her items up. I added mine to hers, offering to pay for our things. She thanked me with a blush, rubbing her arm and looking off into the distance. After I swiped my card and retrieved the receipt, we headed outside. We happened to park right next to one another. I leaned against my car.

"I'm Jalen, by the way. So, tell me—" I paused, hoping she would tell me her name.

"Marisha. Marisha Blackman."

"Marisha, would it be okay if I saw you again after today? I know we just met, but you're beautiful, and I'd love to take you out to dinner or a night on the town."

She smiled but was hesitant. I watched as her lips stretched over her pretty teeth. She was so classy with timeless beauty. It was like she had been on this earth before. Finally, she nodded.

"I would love to. Shall I give you my number?"

"Or I could give you mine. Either way, I plan to call you often," I flirted. "Have you eaten? Would you like me to take you somewhere for a great breakfast and beautiful scenery?"

"Ummm…sure, I'd like that."

We exchanged numbers and hugged. I helped her into her car and then got in mine. She pulled out behind me down the road as I led her downtown to one of the premiere eateries. It was likely bustling with people heading in and out for their morning fix. Although the place was not ridiculously packed, I requested that we sit on the second level balcony. I thanked the waiter and then secretly offered him a tip for his accommodations.

As sucky as my morning had been, Marisha was already making it better.

"If you don't mind me asking, what happened to your face?"

I took a page from her book, lightly touching my face garb and saying, "*Loooong* story. Very, very long story."

She nodded with a tightlipped smile. "So, what do you like to eat here?"

"I always get the meaty skillet with French toast and loaded hash browns," I told her while simultaneously eyeing it on the menu. "In fact, I may order it today."

"Well, I'm not a meat eater," she explained. "But the hash browns sound amazing."

"Oh, really? No meat? Are you a vegetarian?"

"Vegan," she clarified, still looking at the menu. "Basically, I don't eat anything that my family has raised back home in the West Indies. You see so much, living on a farmland and it scars you."

"Aah, I see. So would my meal offend you?"

"Not at all."

We sat in comfortable silence for a moment as she continued to look for what she wanted. The waiter came back after awhile, took our orders, and then gave us complimentary biscuits and butter. She chose not to eat any of it, so I watched her sip on water and suck on a cough drop. For once, my eyes did not wander past a woman's collarbone—seeking to undress her.

Instead, I continued to watch and admire her high cheekbones, eyes, and shy smile. She must not have been used to men staring at her because she ducked her head often and blushed uncontrollably. Even as rich as her skin was, I could see her melanin reddening.

"So how long have you been in America?"

"Almost five years. I spent three years in New York, a year in Chicago, and now I'm here in Waukegan. So far, I've enjoyed the experience, but like I said, I do miss home."

I nodded. "And are you working, or still looking? I know it can be hard sometimes bouncing from place to place and getting adjusted."

"I've been taking on jobs here and there through a temp agency. You know, doing the office assistant thing, and saving up as much as I can in the meantime. My parents send me money every month to hold me over until I can find steady employment," she explained with a small laugh. "I'm also selling my photography online and getting paid for that. My ultimate goal is to model professionally, but so far, no luck."

"I could see you on anyone's magazine. It'll all work out for you, I'm sure."

She smiled. "Thank you. Many people tell me I'm too old to still be pursuing a modeling career, but I'm going after it until it's mine. I've dreamed of it since I was four and now that I'm in America, the opportunity is closer than ever before."

I could smell the determination permeating her. It made me smile that she was so passionate and driven.

"How old are you, if you don't mind me asking?"

"Thirty-one."

Great. I wasn't dealing with an adolescent this time. Although I had over ten years on her, the age difference was not so alarming. She was grown and could make rational, consenting decisions on her own.

"Married?"

"You ask many, many questions, eh?" Her accent came out thickly while she chuckled and shook her head. "But no. No husband. No kids. No responsibilities other than to live the life God intended for me."

"I hear that."

"And *you*? Wife? Kids?"

"No wife or girlfriend. But I have three...I mean, two daughters."

"Why are you confused? You said three and then two," she inquired, looking at me sideways. I couldn't help noticing how her pronunciation of three sounded like tree. It was cute, to say the least.

"I know, I know. I was thinking about the dog I used to own. She was like one of my kids until she passed away," I lied on the spot.

"Oh, you poor thing."

We talked some more about our families and favorite things. We had quite a bit of similarities, but the most important was that she identified as Christian and wanted to develop a deeper relationship with God. I figured we could visit some churches together and hopefully find somewhere we both enjoyed.

By the time we finished eating, talking, and laughing like two old friends, it was almost 11 o'clock and I had completely forgotten about work. I rushed home to email my boss and came up with an excuse and sent it over. I logged into my account shortly after, seeing multiple alerts that potential clients were waiting to be served, but by the time I got to any of them, they expressed that they were no longer interested in meeting. My boss must have been logged into the system as well and saw what was going on because he called me right after.

I spoke into my headset, "Hey, what's up, Dennis?"

"What's up with *you*? You were late logging on, which cost us those few customers."

"Yes, that's my mistake. Something urgent came up and..."

"You should've called me ahead of time and I could have placed someone in your cue," he interjected.

"I know. That's completely my fau..."

"You know my policy, Jalen," he interrupted for a second time. "One customer lost is one too many—let alone *three*."

"I'll work hard to get them back. I promise you."

"I'm afraid it's too late for all of that. I'm going to have to let you go."

"For ONE mistake, Dennis?" I pulled my headset away, looking at it incredulously. Then I positioned it back over my head. "Are you kidding me right now?"

"I wish I was and if we're really tallying mistakes, yours have been costly. You may not see or hear every complaint, but we've had numerous people decline to work with us because you're associated with the brand, and I just can't have you tarnish any more of my hard work. This company was built on integrity and it shall remain so. I'm sorry, Jalen, but..."

"That's evil, Dennis," I hissed. "It's pure evil of you to do that to me. We were close friends before business partners. What kind of thanks is that for a brotha who gave *you* money to start this company? I know I've done wrong in my past but that shouldn't trickle into our business, bro. This is my livelihood. You're *really* firing me—your brother from another mother?"

The line went silent, and I knew I had Dennis thinking. Once upon a time, we were one in the same, and trying to date as many females as we could. We were neck and neck with the numbers in our little black books and had each other's backs through all adversities at one point, so why was he tripping all of a sudden? Why was he judging me out of the blue? He wanted to be high and mighty since he was married, and that's what hurt most. We were all sinners once upon a time, so what made him any different or better than me?

"I see you've forgotten where you come from," I said simply before hanging up.

If he wanted to fire me, then fine. I was not going to beg *anybody* about a job or try to get him to see things differently. I could find something else over the next few weeks. It was in my nature to bounce back, and this time would be no exception.

Chapter Two

I stayed low-key in my spending while I searched for a replacement job. I was only 14 days into unemployment, but I budgeted, cooked more at home instead of going out, and I kept Marisha interested by inviting her to my apartment instead of out on fancy dates.

She was definitely a tough cookie to break. She told me a lot about her life, yet I could tell there was so much more that she was withholding, like why she suddenly left her homeland for America, and why she had moved so frequently within the last few years. Marisha was special nonetheless and I found myself looking forward to her calls and text messages each day.

We were going dancing downstairs later this evening. Our apartment clubhouse put on events every month for its residents, so salsa dancing was on this month's itinerary. Marisha claimed she did not know how to dance, but she was from the islands. Surely, she could shake *something*. As I went into the freezer to grab the ice tray, I caught the flyer on my refrigerator and realized today was my ex-wife's book signing.

I went over a few scenarios in my head on whether or not I should go. Would she dismiss me and 'curse' me for coming? Would I upset her by showing my face? Or would she be thankful to see me? Our last conversation over six years ago ended on okay terms; I apologized to her, on my hands and knees while crying, and told her that I still loved her. Of course, mentally, physically, and emotionally she was in an entirely different place and would not take me back. Although so many years had gone by since then, that still did not mean she wanted to ever see me again. At the same time, I wanted to show my support and purchase a copy of the book. I had done her wrong for so long *then* that it would only be right to support her in her dreams *now*.

I had another hour and a half before it began and looked for an appropriate outfit that I could wear to the book signing and also keep on for salsa dancing. I decided on a simple satin black shirt. I left two buttons open, splaying the top of my chest and the baby fine hairs that were there. Dark grey slacks and black suede loafers completed the ensemble. A single gold chain and gold pinky ring were my only splashes of color. I tucked the flyer in my back pocket but not before drenching myself in cologne. I also brushed my hair so that the soft waves on top looked presentable and neat.

It was time to encounter my past.

As I headed out of the door, I tripped over a bag of clothes and a backpack that seemed like it held bricks inside.

"What in the world?" I questioned, stepping over what I presumed to be trash or one of my neighbor's belongings. "Hello?"

I looked around but saw no one. Then, out of nowhere, I heard and saw a woman struggling to bring up other bags of clothes and household items. Behind her were two figures with hoods on their heads. As she finally neared my apartment, she threw the items down to the floor and dusted off her hands. It was Rochelle, the mother of my children. My daughters followed behind her, their heads low and their faces stained with tears.

"So, you show up after I've been contacting you for months to see my kids?" I questioned her, still confused as to why she was bringing bags to my place. A typical weekend visit only warranted a small duffel bag that both girls put their belongings in. "What's going on with you?"

"I don't have to answer any questions from you. You aren't my man nor are you my father. You're barely a good co-parent."

"Rochelle, are you serious? You don't let me see my kids! All I can do is send money and get a text every blue moon." I stepped out of the way as she flung a smaller bag in my direction. "And what's all this trash?"

"This *trash* is our daughter's school clothes, summer clothes, and winter clothes! Their shoes are in the blue bag, and I've packed up their medications for their allergies and eczema. Figure it out, Jalen! I'm tired of doing this on my own!" she yelled.

"What are you talking about? Doing what on your own? Answer me, Rochelle!"

I watched as she threw her hands in the air as if she had had enough of life itself, snarled, and then turned to our daughters. She hugged them both and then began whispering to them. Was this what I thought it was? Was she really dropping the kids off to stay with me for a few weeks? Going off of these bags, it seemed like it would be a couple months or even *permanently*. But I knew that could not be the case.

I softened my voice. "What's going on, Chelle? Why are you crying and acting all hysterical?"

She never answered me. She kissed our 15-year-old daughters on the cheeks, handed me an inhaler inside of a snack bag that was labeled *Autumn*, and then turned and walked away without another word. I let her go. Maybe the girls would explain what was going on with their mother. I motioned for them to grab their bags and follow me inside my apartment, while I held the door open and pushed a few in myself. Once everything was inside, I leaned against the counter and looked at them standing in the middle of the room.

"I've got to say. I wasn't expecting you, but I'm happy to see you. How have you two been?"

Autumn just looked at me with a growing attitude while Summer tugged on her side ponytail uncomfortably. I raised my eyebrows and pressed my lips together. No one said anything.

"*Hellooo?*" I waved my hands sarcastically and stood to my full height. "How are you? Autumn? Summer? Can you say hi to your dad? Give me a hug or something. I haven't seen you girls in so long."

"And that's *our* fault?" Autumn questioned. She was always the hothead of the two, like her mother. "Hey, Daddy. How are things going in your selfish little world? Is that what you want to hear? It's not like you deserve the title."

"Autumn, stop it," Summer scolded her sister softly, leaning into me for an awkward hug.

"Nah, he needs to hear this. That's why Mom hates him now. He was barely around when we were little, and he's barely around now."

I closed my eyes briefly and then exhaled. "Little girl, don't be disrespectful. Your mother took away a lot of my visiting privileges when she moved out. I wanted to see and be there for you two, but your mother didn't want me there. Don't act like that. You know I love you both."

Autumn rolled her eyes and stomped her foot. Summer sighed and shoved her hands in her pockets. They were polar opposites and had been that way since they were little. Autumn had short, kinky curls, and Summer wore her hair mostly in long braids going to the back of her head. Autumn was more developed physically for her age, while Summer looked like a little girl for the most part. Autumn's personality was sassy and bold, while Summer lacked confidence. Although identical twins, they had a ton of differences.

"Are you girls hungry? Did your mom feed you?"

Summer played with the charms on her bracelet. "We just ate some cereal this morning, but that's it."

"What would you like to eat? I was on my way to the mall. We could stop at the food court and pick up some burgers or tacos, or something."

"We don't eat beef or pork. You would know that if you were around us more!" Autumn snapped.

I ignored her and told them to come on. I did not have time for catty adolescent talk. Besides, their mother had obviously brainwashed them to think that I did not want to be in their lives, and I was going to have to debunk all those myths before the weekend ended and Rochelle returned for the girls.

We headed out and I made small talk with Summer while Autumn sat with her arms crossed and pouted. She looked out of the window with her lip poked out and I was reminded of when she was a little girl, throwing a tantrum. I couldn't help but laugh as I stared at her in the rearview. She looked up and caught my eyes, frowning more. My gaze bounced back and forth between the road and her pouty face, until she finally gave in and laughed along with me. My heart warmed instantly. That was my girl.

"Look at my baby smiling. I've missed that smile. Can we at least agree to have a good weekend and enjoy this time we have together?"

They both spoke in unison, "Yes."

"All right. That's what I'm talking about."

We drove the remainder of the way to the mall, singing, laughing, and talking as if we had never been apart from each other. When we made it to the Waukegan Shopping Plaza, I gave the girls 25 dollars and told them to stay at the booth nearest the bookstore.

"While y'all eat, I'm going to go next door and pick up a book, okay? Don't talk to anybody, and don't move. If I'm still in there by the time you're done, come find me. Do I make myself clear?" I instructed, watching them chow down on the fried rice and veggie egg rolls they had gotten from a Chinese restaurant.

"Mmhmm," they mumbled in between bites.

"Alright. I'll be back," I promised, winking and strolling next door.

There was a bit of a line as I headed into the bookstore, looking around for Jamaika. I saw a backdrop with her image and book cover on it. There was also a table draped in a black cloth with rich, crimson rose petals splayed atop it. There were also stacks and stacks of her books, a collection of pens, bookmarks, business cards, and other promotional materials. It was overwhelming but in a great way. I could not believe this was actually happening for her.

I careened my neck around the semi-busy bookstore, finally catching Jamaika as she came from the back of the store with a sign tucked under her arm. The long line of potential new readers and supporters cheered lightly as she waved and greeted them. She walked with who I assumed was her husband. I take that back. I *knew* for a fact that he was her husband, and they were very much in love because of the way he watched her roll out her sign and hang it up to her liking. He stood back, nodding and approving where she placed the sign. He seemed to be in awe of her confidence and the way she took over, speaking with a few readers who had come early, and expressing her concerns to the sales associate.

Jamaika wore a dress that was intricately designed. It was fitting and hung just above her knees. On one of the shoulders of the dress was a large glittery flower. She wore tall heels and silver accessories. Obviously, she was doing well because I could see the glistening diamonds from where I stood. Her hair was pinned up and red lipstick—that perfectly matched the rose petals on her table—made her lips desirable.

I leaned onto a bookshelf, looking at her husband who was dressed casually in a red polo shirt, Khaki shorts, and overpriced black and red tennis shoes from some renowned athlete. He had a cap turned backwards on his head and a few tattoos of crosses and scriptures on his forearm. The biggest tattoo, nestled just below his visible bicep, caught my attention immediately and read *Jamaika*.

In his arms was a young girl with two long braids down the sides of her head. Following behind them was a boy around eight or nine with designs shaved neatly on the side of his head. Both children were a perfect mixture of the two. Then, my heart dropped even more as my former mother-in-law,

Stella, came out of the back of the store. She pushed a set of twins out in a stroller who were no older than two or three years old. They, too, looked just like Jamaika and her husband.

My ex-wife had *four* children...a set of twins at that. With me, we could never conceive. Even more amazing was that she had extremely young children, but her body looked like it had not birthed a single child. Overall, she was more stunning than I ever remembered her. It blew my mind as I continued to stare until I knocked a few books off the shelf. The sound of the books hitting the floor caused a majority of heads to turn my way, including my ex-wife. I could have smacked myself as I leaned to pick them up and then smiled uneasily.

"Hello," I spoke, nodding towards Jamaika.

"*Jalen?*" She squinted, putting the pen she held down and walking over cautiously. "Oh, my God. Is that you?"

"It's me." I smiled.

Instead of rolling her eyes or dismissing me, she opened her arms and gave me a brief hug. It was one of those church hugs where you didn't know the person well but wanted to let them know you cared in Jesus's name. It felt rehearsed and unnatural, and I could smell her fragrance on me as she pulled away.

"You look amazing," I whispered against her hair.

"Thanks! But um...what are you doing here?"

"Yeah," her husband spoke up this time, placing their daughter on her feet. "What *are* you doing here? I don't recall anyone personally inviting you."

I held up the flyer that had been placed in my mailbox. "I just wanted to support the future best-selling author. I can leave if you'd like. I don't mean any harm."

"You're fine," Jamaika told me and then turned to her husband, "Baby, relax. I'm okay. Take the kids to get some ice cream or something."

"Nah, we're fine, sitting here."

I bit on the inside of my cheek and smirked. His little attitude was cute. He wanted to show me who was the man, and I could respect that.

"Is something funny?" he asked, noticing my amused look.

"Nothing's funny. I'm just amazed at where God has taken her." I pulled out my wallet and gave her a ten-dollar bill and five-dollar bill. "May I have an autographed copy?"

Jamaika accepted the money, her eyes lighting up. I did not necessarily think she was smitten by my gesture, but she was definitely surprised that I had shown up and bought a book.

"Let me get your change," she announced.

I assumed the books were twelve or thirteen dollars and waved my hand in dismissal. "Keep it."

"Thank you, Jay," my nickname that she called me once upon a time slipped out, sounding like music to my ears. She leaned over to sign the book, and I studied her body as I reminisced on the sexual things we did once upon a time.

Her husband—whatever his name was—cleared his throat. He must have seen where my eyes landed. I continued to ignore him and stared at her son, who walked up and pressed his cheek against her arm.

"Momma, I'm tired. When will this be over?"

"Baby, give me just a few hours, and then we can drive back home and relax all weekend."

I wondered where she lived as I watched her finish signing the book and then walk back over to me. Shyly, she tucked a piece of hair behind her ear and then placed the book in my hands. She smiled, whispered a *"thanks, Jay,"* and then said nothing more as she turned around and walked back over to her family. By now, more people were pouring in and the signing was officially on. I was glad I had arrived when I did.

"Take care," I called out.

She only acknowledged me with a final wave and then sat down in her seat, ready to network and wow people with her grace and beauty. This authoring thing was going to be a success for her; I just knew it. I nodded to her husband, who surprisingly nodded back, and that was that. I had encountered my past for a final time, made peace, and could move on.

Chapter Three

I went to retrieve the girls and we grabbed ice cream before leaving the mall. When I showed them the back of the book where Jamaika's picture was, they vaguely remembered her. It made sense; my girls were young when we divorced. I sent Rochelle a few text messages to see when she would be back to get the girls, not that I was ready for them to leave. I just wanted to know. We drove around the city, went to the park, took a few selfies on my phone, and talked about their teenage problems. Thankfully no mention of boys was in that conversation.

We headed home to the sounds of some pop star singing that they both loved. Meanwhile, I cringed the entire time.

"When did your mother say she'd be back?" I asked no one in particular, pulling up into my apartment complex.

"She didn't say," Summer chimed in.

"Oh, okay. She hasn't answered any of my messages. Guess I'll try again tomorrow."

We headed up to the third floor and as I opened the door, I received the shock of my life. From wall to wall, my things had been ransacked and thrown around. It literally looked like a raid by the police or mafia.

"What happened, Dad?" Autumn asked, looking panicked. "Who did this?"

"I don't know," I mumbled, gritting my teeth and stepping further inside. "Girls, stay right here while I check the place."

I turned on all the lights and went around in each room to make sure no one was still lurking inside. When the coast was clear, I told the girls to sit down in the living room and gave them my iPad to keep them occupied. I took pictures of my bathroom and the explicit words written in the shower in lipstick and permanent marker. The words *WOMANIZER, HYPOCRITE, JERK,* and *YOU ARE THE FATHER* were written in shaving cream around my bedroom walls. A sad face made of cherries sat on my bed.

Every room grew worse and worse, it seemed. Mirrors were broken, my underwear was ripped and bleached, and it appeared that a mini fire had been started and then put out in the bathtub, along with some of my suit jackets. I was especially angry that one of my 50-inch TVs had a high heel lodged in it. The girls' belongings were unscathed.

I recorded a video of myself telling the date, time, and location. This had Kyla written all over it. She was the only one with a key and who claimed I fathered her baby. She had probably come back to start some mess with me. In a way, I was glad I was gone when she came. There was no telling what or who she had brought with her—namely, her husband.

I called the police and filed a break-in report, noting that no items had been stolen but were just thrashed. I also told them who I suspected it might be. The responder chuckled over the phone; he told me this was not the first incident today where a scorned lover had messed up someone's belongings.

This woman was psychotic. I realized she was upset that I had put my hands on her, but she was playing with fire now. She had messed up my apartment, and I would likely not receive my security deposit back once I moved. I'm sure her fingerprints were all over the place, or a strand of hair, or something that could be used to incriminate her later on down the line.

Two male police officers arrived a half-hour later. One took pictures and wrote down a few illegible sentences on a yellow notepad. The other asked me over 100 questions, it seemed, before apologizing that my belongings had been damaged. They promised to investigate the situation further. They left me with a business card and a pat on the shoulder.

"You guys take care," I called out, closing the door behind them. I did not lock it because I knew I'd have to make a few runs to the trashcans downstairs. I sighed and turned back around to face the madness. It was time to clean up this mess. "Girls, can you do me a favor?"

"Yes," they answered in unison.

I never got around to telling them my request because the door opened behind me. The building manager and the owner of the property stood before me. Their eyebrows were sky-high in shock as they entered without my permission and looked around.

"What in the world happened to my place?" the owner cried out, taking off his baseball cap and slamming it down to the floor. He gripped his baldhead with both hands and grew cherry red. I was convinced that smoke seeped from his ears like a cartoon character.

"Calm down, Chad! This wasn't my doing," I rushed to explain. "Please let me tell you the full story."

"Mr. Owens, you have two minutes to tell me why my apartment is in shambles. What is going on in my building?" he asked a little calmer this time, but he spoke through gritted teeth. "I've gotten multiple complaints over the last several weeks, and today I get a call from my buddy who works at the police department that was called out to your apartment."

I decided honesty was the best policy and told him the truth. That's what I taught my girls, even if I'd previously not done it. Lying would only make matters worse. "A woman I used to date came and ransacked the place while I wasn't home."

As soon as the words touched the atmosphere, I knew I'd messed up. Chad's face grew pale in disbelief. He stumbled over his words, clearly stumped by my violation of his apartment rules.

"If she came while you were gone, then that means she must have had a key. Your lease states that only *one* key is given per person, according to household size. There is only ONE person listed on your lease and that's *you*, so not only did you violate your lease agreement, but you made a copy of a key that should not have been duplicated." He went from pale to as red as a tomato, spewing, "Jalen, that's illegal!"

I could feel the anxiety pouring on thicker and thicker. I had an idea where this conversation was going, but I hoped he wasn't as heartless as I thought he was.

"Chad, I—I…I can't say sorry enough. I truly apologize for this, and I promise I'll pay for the damages if you just…"

My landlord held his hand up to stop me. "Jalen, I took a chance on you. You KNEW my hesitations with allowing you to rent from me. This is a building with a majority of elderly residents, and drama and disturbances are the LAST things I wanted my residents to experience."

"I understand that, and I'm sorry for disturbing—"

Chad closed his fiery eyes in frustration. "Save your apologies for another landlord at another property. You have one week from today to get your stuff out of my building. I can't afford to have you bring down my property value and bring unrest to the community. I like you, man, but you need to get it together. There's been nothing but a trail of trouble following you."

"Chad, come on, man! Don't do me like this. I—I've got my daughters with me!"

My pleas obviously fell on deaf ears as Chad took a few steps back, shaking his head.

"I'm sorry." He shrugged. "It's out of my hands. If a majority of my residents are upset and unhappy, then I must get rid of the common denominator…and that would be *you*," he explained.

I just stared at him, hoping that this was some sort of dream. I looked back to my girls who were listening in on our conversation. Their expressions showed apprehension, and quite frankly, I was worried too. My gift of gab, at this point, wasn't going to save me from this impending misfortune. I guess I really had lost my touch.

"So, you're going to toss my kids and I out on the streets? Is that what you're saying? You have children, don't you, Chad? How would you feel if you and your children were thrown out of a home?"

"I wouldn't put my children in that situation. It's simple."

"But what about…?"

"ENOUGH! Mr. Owens…*one* week," was all Chad said. He gave me a final glare, turned and walked out.

When I was sure that he was long gone and out of earshot, I screamed out as loud as I could, and then beat my fists against the door. My girls stood in shock as I got out all of my frustration by yelling and beating up the door. I was adding more damage to my apartment but at that point, I had nothing to lose…*literally*. Everything was completely going downhill and spiraling so far out of control that I could not keep up. It was overwhelming, to say the least.

I decided to clean up my bedroom and bathroom until both spaces were spotless and then made a pallet on the floor. I ordered takeout and we watched a movie that they suggested. I told the girls to lie in my bed while I took the floor. As sleep threatened to take over, we prayed together and then shared a few *I love you*s.

As my girls fell into peaceful slumber, I knew it would be a while before I joined them. I could not help but to stare up at the ceiling and wonder what was next. What more could possibly go wrong? Was I *that* terrible of a person that karma had to hit me all at once, and bring my daughters down with me? I had been thrown out of a church that I favored; I'd lost my job, hit a woman out of anger, been accused of fathering a child, and lost my apartment all within a couple of weeks.

The weekend came to an end, and as much as I hated to see my daughters leave, I also knew that I did not want them to be part of any other drama or foolishness that came my way. I texted their mother to ask her if she would be picking them up or if I needed to drop them off but received no answer. This seemed to be the theme of the weekend; I could see that she read my messages, but she never responded or returned any of my calls either. I knew she was upset with me for whatever reason, but she had no right to bring our kids into it. We still had to have open communication when it came to co-parenting, and that was something she was always terrible at doing.

"Does your mom have another phone or something?"

Autumn shook her head. We were getting dressed and ready for the day. I brushed my teeth and looked back and forth between them, wondering if they knew something I didn't.

"Well, we will grab breakfast and then you two can show me where she lives now. I'll drop you both off in a little bit, okay?" I spoke with toothpaste in my mouth.

They nodded. Summer sat in between Autumn's legs, while her hair was braided. I smiled at the image and disappeared back into the bathroom. I had the gumption to check social media to see what Rochelle was up to. Once upon a time, she was the queen of taking pictures, and had become a slave to a few likes and followers on Facebook and Instagram. Surely, she had posted something with her new man.

As I looked on her page, there were an unimaginable number of pictures that people had tagged her in. I figured she was a bridesmaid this weekend to one of her loud-mouthed friends because there were six other women that she posed with at a restaurant and some sort of karaoke bar. They wore sashes and all white attire and had on party hats and pins.

As I scrolled further, I nearly lost my grip on the phone and I began to choke at the sight of her dressed in a wedding gown. Images of her man in a tuxedo with his groomsmen popped up. I could see in the background of several pictures a breathtaking view of a beach, and a church stationed on a few acres of sandy shores. I zoomed in on one of the pictures to see the name of the church and then searched it online. Google revealed that the church was located in Saint Thomas.

I dropped the phone altogether and cringed as it crashed to the tile floor. Rochelle had flown out and gotten married this weekend. Not only had she gotten married, but she had also left our daughters out of the ceremony, which let me know this was all premeditated. She knew what she was doing when she dropped them off out of the blue and did not offer me any explanation. She had purposely left out those details, knowing I would have protested the wedding. She did not know her "husband" well—all she saw was money and an opportunity.

Summer rushed in, hearing the noise my phone made. "Daddy, you okay?"

I knelt down to grab the phone and checked it to make sure there were no scratches or cracks. "I'm good, baby girl. You girls ready to rock and roll?"

"Let's roll, Daddy."

I decided not to even discuss the findings about their mother. Unlike Rochelle, I wasn't comfortable planting seeds of hatred in their spirit like she had done with me. Obviously, she wasn't going to be able to pick them up since she was away, eloping, but I would have to come up with some sort of explanation as to why their mother wasn't coming back or returning calls. I sent Rochelle a message on Facebook, chastising her, and then logged off for the day.

We headed to my favorite breakfast spot— the same spot I had taken Marisha on our first official date, and then it dawned on me. With all that was going on with my apartment, I had stood her up the night before. We were supposed to go dancing and I had forgotten to cancel our date. Hopefully she wasn't mad at me and would understand my situation. As we settled in one of the booths, I gave her a call.

She did not answer on the first or second ring. She answered after the fourth. Expecting to hear her soft, sweet voice, I was taken aback by the brash, commanding tone in my ear.

"Yeah. Who is this?"

"Uuhh," I stuttered for a moment. "It's, um, Jay—Marisha's friend."

"*Marisha?* You've got the wrong number, my dude. There's no person by that name," the caller said and then hung up.

Okay, now I was confused. I stared at the phone, knowing it was the same number that I had gotten from Marisha, and the same number we texted and called from on a number of occasions. I was puzzled but put the phone down and figured I would address that at another time. My girls were hungry and ready to order.

"Dad, did you ever hear back from Momma?"

"No." I shook my head, looking over at Summer. "She never answered my calls or texts, sweetheart."

"I wonder what's up with her? She was acting so weird all week. Said something about a new start," Autumn mumbled, shrugging.

"New start, huh?"

If only they knew what Rochelle was really hinting about. I checked my phone again, logging onto Facebook. I went straight to Rochelle's page but received an error message. The message was telling me that I no longer had access to the page. I refreshed my browser and then tried to look at her page again. I received the same message. *User Not Found.* Had she blocked me? Did she see my message and decide to block me from seeing any other posts?

I went to her other social media pages and sure enough, she had blocked and banned me from all forms of contacting her. I attempted to call and text her, but it was apparent that she had completely erased me from her life in just a few hours. Why would she do that if I had the girls with me? How would she contact me so that I could drop them back off and communicate with her on future visits? How would I know when she returned from out of the country? Or better yet, *did* she plan on returning? Did she bring me all the girls' bags of clothes because she did not plan on coming back and being a mother? If she could elope and leave her kids out of an important decision like marriage, then I would not put anything past Rochelle anymore.

Perspiration coated my forehead as I tried to calm down from having a breakdown right then and there. I needed answers and I needed them immediately. With unemployment as my reality and the world turned against me, there was no way I could survive without Rochelle's help as a single parent. She needed to be in her daughters' lives for obvious reasons, but also because there was no way I could raise them on my own.

They weren't children, by any means, but they still needed that mother figure. Who would teach them about their menstrual cycles and wearing bras? Who would teach them how to cook and carry themselves like women? Who was going to teach them how to be future wives and mothers, what makeup to wear, and how to style their hair?

I shoved the straw past my lips and downed the complimentary water until the glass was dry, breathing heavily. Still, I could not seem to catch my breath or quench my thirst.

"Dad, you alright? You're sweating."

"Yeah, I'm…I'm alright, girls," I assured them with a smile but deep down inside, I was losing it. Life had *officially* spun out of control.

Chapter Four

Just as Chad requested, the girls and I moved out within seven days. I gave no warning to my neighbors and did not even try to clean up as best I could since I knew I would not be receiving any security deposit from the mess that Kyla made. We would be staying at one of the long-term stay hotels, nestled in downtown Waukegan. Although the room was nice and beautiful, and I'd be saving a couple hundred bucks a month, the space just wasn't ideal for three people. The girls were just as disappointed and confused, but it would have to do for now. We moved and settled in as best we could, and figured this was now life, as we knew it.

I still had yet to hear back from Marisha, and I definitely had more questions about the guy that answered the phone. Had she been caught in a lie? Was this somebody she was seeing? Was this the husband she said she didn't have? I would never know. I did not plan on calling the number back or questioning her about it, but if we ever crossed paths, I expected some sort of an explanation. I had developed feelings for her. They were fresh and new, but they were feelings, nonetheless. She seemed like such a decent girl and yet she was nowhere to be found. But I could no longer concern myself with that foolishness. I had to move on from whatever it was we had.

I stood in front of the bathroom mirror now, securing my bowtie with a concentrated look on my face. I was normally a pro at doing these things, but today, my nerves were shot. I had landed a job interview at a marketing firm that paid just as much as my previous job. The only difference is I would be working at an actual office and not from the comforts of home. Either way, I wanted and needed the job badly and said a silent prayer as I finished getting dressed. I ordered the girls a little room service and told them to stay put while I went and aced the interview.

"Good luck, Dad!" they called out in unison.

I checked my bank account like I had done religiously for the last several weeks. I was almost down to my last. The vegetarian pizza that I ordered for the girls had put me in the double digits now. I needed this job like *yesterday*. An employment check was coming next week, so I had no idea what we would do between now and next Friday.

As I made my way to my car, I said a prayer. I said another prayer as I headed to the building where the interview would take place, and right up until I was called in back, my thoughts were on the Lord making a way out of no way. I know I had not been the most faithful servant, but hopefully, God would see my heart. I was truly trying, and most importantly, I had hit rock bottom. I had nothing and no one else besides my girls—I *needed* this position.

"Come on in, Mr. Owens," I was summoned from the doorway by who I assumed was the supervisor or assistant supervisor. He just looked to be in control and a person with authority. "Have a seat."

I offered a hand and smiled. "How are you doing today, Mr....?"

"Have a seat," the man repeated and ignored my gesture to shake his hand and get his full name. Under different circumstances, I would have given him a piece of my mind, but I needed this job and could not mess up my chances.

I did as he demanded and took a seat across from him. He was a big guy with piercing dark eyes, broad shoulders that were clearly tense, and a disposition that scared me half to death. He wore a black suit jacket with a cream-colored shirt beneath. A splash of red from his bowtie completed his ensemble. He was stern looking, and apparently, had an attitude problem.

"Is…everything okay?" I questioned, palming the manila folder that housed my two-page resume.

"I'm good. *You*, on the other hand, seem so tense." The man sized me up with a crooked smile. There was something about his eyes that I didn't like. "Loosen up, man. Breathe a little. Can I get you anything? Water? Coffee? Tea? Ice?"

"*Ice*? Why would I need ice?"

"Wild guess." The man, whose name I still didn't know, swiveled around in his chair and crossed a leg comfortably. He had a smug look. "Let's just get to the point, shall we? Do you even know why you're here today, man?"

"Uh, yeah. I'm going to take a *wild guess* and say it's to interview for the position I applied for. Am I right?" If he wanted to be sarcastic and condescending, so could I.

He pointed a finger at me, leaning forward. "Let's get one thing straight. I don't like you. I never have liked you. And it's likely I never will like you."

"You don't even know me. How professional is this?" I sat forward, loosening the bowtie around my neck. I suddenly felt warm, as anger pumped through my veins.

The guy slammed a burly hand down on the desk and then stood up. He rounded his desk, approaching me. I stood up to my full height, staring him eye to eye. He didn't look familiar, and I hardly ever forgot a face, so I was still confused by his assessment of me. He chuckled at my boldness and then pushed me so hard that I collided with the wall behind me. My head slammed into a painting, causing it to crash to the floor. He took the liberty of pressing a button on the phone, paging his secretary.

"Marisha, hold all my calls, please."

Marisha. Marisha. Was that who I thought it was? I had not seen her on my way in, but it was a rare name in this small town and a rare name in general. I didn't have much time to think about it because I was being charged up again.

"Get up," the man ordered, standing above me with clenched fists.

I was not a small guy by any means, but he made me feel that way as he stared down at me. Reluctantly, I regained my footing and rubbed the back of my head.

"Do you know who I am?" he demanded, breathing heavily.

"No. Should I?"

"I'm Kyla's husband!" he barked, throwing a single punch and catching me by surprise. Again, I fell to the floor like a ragdoll. I was well over 200 pounds, but the way he handled me, one would think I was much lighter. He threw another jab, and then another, causing my jaw to make a weird cracking sound. Hopefully it was not broken because much like his wife, he packed a heck of a punch. At this rate, my face would never properly heal.

"I should kill you right here and now for putting your hands on my wife. Not only that, but I should make you disappear for even raising your voice at her. She told me everything, and I've been on a manhunt to find you ever since. It just so happens the same guy who I've been searching for applied to *my* company," he explained. "You think it's okay to lie down with other people's wives? Just who do you think you are?"

There was nothing I could say. He had me and I was a fool to have done those things, but what could I do? I had an angry, irate man staring me down and there was no way of escape other than turning my back to him, which I definitely knew not to do.

He knelt down in front of me and patted my swollen jaw with his hand twice. He smirked as I coughed up blood. "Listen up and listen closely. Before all this supervisor stuff, I was a pretty well-known drug lord who could make a person disappear like this." He snapped his fingers. "The Lord saved me but He ain't done with me yet. I could easily add another number to my body count."

"Is that a threat?" I questioned, feeling blood ooze from my nostrils.

"Oh no, no, Jalen." He leaned in so close that I smelled the hatred *and* stench on his breath. He cupped the back of my neck in his large hand and tightened it until I could no longer breathe. Only when I began to get dizzy and feel faint did he release my neck from his hold. He continued, "It's not a threat at all. It's a promise. Don't ever talk to my wife again. Don't ever text her. As a matter of fact, delete her number and if you ever see her on the streets, look the other way. Otherwise, the next time we run into each other will be at *your* funeral. I'll make sure of it. Do you hear me?"

I assumed I did not answer quickly enough, so he pressed his thumb into my left eye. "I got it! I got it! Yes. I hear you," I pleaded, my body going limp for a moment. I blinked away the swirling stars in my eyes and tried not to succumb to the flashing light. "I'm sorry!"

"Get out," was all he said above a whisper.

I did not need to be told twice. I scrambled on all fours for a moment, trying to stand. When I finally had enough strength and understanding of my surroundings, I staggered along the wall, until I reached the door. It felt extra heavy as I opened it and literally ran out. I nearly knocked the secretary over. It was no longer the blonde, petite woman I saw originally. Marisha stood, holding papers in her hands and looking worried as she took in my bloody face and disheveled appearance.

"Your face. Oh, my goodness. What happened?" she asked softly. "Do you need an ambulance?"

"You knew about this! You were in on this all along," I accused her, brushing her hand from my face. "Don't touch me!"

She genuinely looked concerned as she looked me over and tried to reach again for my face. "What are you talking about? I didn't know about anything!"

I ignored her and did not stop running until I reached the parking structure. Once inside my car, I drove off with the sound of burning rubber echoing throughout the structure. I sped the entire way home and then ducked my head as I walked past the girls. They were into a TV show, giggling and talking about some woman's questionable fashion choices, and did not notice me walking past briskly, thank God. I definitely didn't want them to see me bloody, battered and at my worse, for obvious reasons.

I headed to my room, closed the door, and cried. It was not just tears flowing from my eyes but one of those ugly, come-to-Jesus-moment cries. My throat actually formed a sound, and I could not catch my breath. What could possibly go wrong next? Tears coated my eyes so much that I could not see in front of me but somehow, I managed to find my way to my bookshelf where I grabbed the book that Jamaika had written. I decided right then and there was the time to read it. It was like I was drawn to the book; God was trying to tell me something, and I was perilous not to take heed.

I skimmed over her first few pages—it was a bunch of different acknowledgments of people in our previous circle and many others that I did not know. She included a scripture at the very end of her "thank yous" and there was a picture of her family, whom she dedicated the book to. Even with my wounded, throbbing face, a smile caused my lips to curl up slightly as tears continued to fall past my cheekbones. My shirt would be dripping wet by the time this cry was over. It was like I couldn't stop. The stress was too much. The events were frequent. I needed a break from the bad news, seriously.

I paged and read through Jamaika detailing the first 17 years of her life before she met me. To protect my identity, she referred to me as "Jason" but everybody in our town would know whom she was talking about. We were once a power couple and people to be envied. As twisted as our marriage was, we were still local celebrities, and everyone wanted what we had.

Sitting on the edge of the bed, I read her intimate thoughts about how she had met her

Prince Charming but as time went on, my hands were no longer gentle, and my words were no longer encouraging. I read on in silent sadness as she detailed how often I would cheat on her and abuse her, and said that no matter how hard she tried, she could not please me. She told readers how much she cried and caked on makeup after our violent encounters, and how she avoided public places days at a time while her face and body healed. She even mentioned that she stopped counting when I'd hit her for the 200th time. Had it really been that many times?

I nearly dropped the book in my shaky, clammy hands as she went on to share her suicide attempt with readers and how coldly I reacted by bringing my mistress to the hospital room to check up on her. Was I really that evil? Was I really this heartless monster she described with so much passion and pain? Maybe there really was a Jason, because surely, I wasn't this terrible of a husband.

I read about her miscarriages and realized I had caused one. I had choked and slammed her against the wall, one night, after dinner with friends because she embarrassed me. I remembered that night well, but had no idea she was pregnant at the time. This was something she never told me. I had killed my own seed. I grew sick at the thought of it, slamming the book shut and throwing it against the wall. I proceeded to slam my balled fists against the wall, not caring who heard me.

I was not angry at her decision to write a tell-all book and be freed from the turmoil I brought to her life. I was outraged at how horrible I had been to her. I was furious that I left her and allowed another man to come in and take my wife. I was upset that I was so dumb, irresponsible, and misguided back then. Thankfully, she didn't look like what she had been through, but I had still caused her woes and that was something that "sorry" could not fix.

One of the girls entered and asked if I was okay. I nodded, never turning around and showing my face. After all, how would I explain my tearstained face, nearly broken jaw and nose, red eyes, and now bruised knuckles? How would I tell my daughter that not only was I her father, but a woman beater, adulterer, and child killer? I wasn't the superhero or cool father anymore; I was the man with many skeletons in his closet. I was ashamed to be me in that moment. The thought rocked me as I slumped over, falling to my knees.

I needed help and fast. I couldn't breathe. I couldn't catch my breath or gather my footing properly. It was like I was falling hundreds of feet and no matter where I grabbed or reached, I continued to fall into a dark pit. Was I dying? Was this my own personal hell consuming me?

"Daddy!"

I heard Summer or Autumn's sweet voice. In my panic, I could not decipher who was speaking. All I could do was whisper, "Get Daddy some help."

No sooner than my lips popped with the letter "P" did everything around me turn black. Maybe I *was* dead. Who knows? I deserved it either way.

Chapter Five

When I came to, I heard the sounds of rhythmic beeping, faint talking from voices I didn't know, and weeping. Where was I? My eyes were swollen shut and felt sore. The last thing I remembered was falling...and before that, I remembered crying so hard that my tear ducts were tender. Perhaps this is why my face felt puffy and stiff. I attempted to open my eyes but could not. I attempted to talk, but I literally could not find the words. It felt like my throat was on fire. So, I just moved my hands, hoping someone saw me. I heard a gasp.

"Daddy, you're up!" my daughters both screamed in unison. Then it dawned on me; I was in a hospital room.

A few moments passed before I heard another presence in the room—likely a nurse or doctor. My vitals were checked, and medical tape was gently pulled from my eyes. That would explain why I could not open them. I looked around, slowly getting adjusted to the light while blinking away the stickiness in the corners of my eyes. My daughters had a look of concern on their faces. I focused on the woman standing in front of me.

"Welcome back, Mr. Owens."

The nurse gave an empathetic smile as she instructed me to cough. I did as told, feeling a quick pull from my throat. I had a tube down my throat, which now explained why everything seemed to burn internally. I coughed several more moments involuntarily, catching my breath. I was given a cup of ice but was told I could only suck the little bit of water from the straw.

"Don't attempt to chew on the ice. You may choke," the young, brown-skinned woman emphasized. "Are you okay while I go grab the doctor?"

I nodded, thanking her with my watery eyes. She disappeared and I looked to my daughters, hoping to offer some kind of comfort, but instead, they showered *me* with cautious hugs and tearful kisses. I showed them as much love as my weakened body would allow before a doctor entered and interrupted our moment.

"Good evening. I'm Dr. Mathias. How are you feeling? Give a thumbs up for okay, and a thumbs down for not okay."

I gave him a thumbs up. Truthfully, I felt all right other than needing a throat lozenge to clear the scratchiness in my throat.

"Glad to hear," he continued. "Mr. Owens, I assume you have no idea why you're here, or did Nurse Rekhia explain it a bit to you?"

I shook my head no.

He went on, tucking a pen behind his ear. "You suffered a mild stroke that we can only assume was brought on by insurmountable amounts of stress. Otherwise, you were a picture of perfect health, beyond your physical wounds."

That was the last thing I imagined he would say. My heart dropped. Previous family members and church members had experienced strokes and never fully recovered. Some had even succumbed to it. Would this be my fate? Would I lose the ability to walk or talk, or do normal things like drive and run?

Dr. Mathias seemed to pick up on the uncertainty on my face. "We are running tests to get to the bottom of it, but I can assure you that you will make a FULL recovery as the stroke was caught in the preliminary stages. You have your daughters to thank for calling 911 and perfectly describing your location and symptoms to the dispatcher."

I looked over at my daughters, winking as best as I could. Even my eyelids hurt.

"Right now, I'm sure you feel a little out of it so I'm going to let you rest. You also have a semi-fractured jaw that I will assume came about when you fell to the floor, and there is significant swelling to your nose and temple, but with time, that'll subside. If you need anything, please don't hesitate to press the call button. We'll also be getting food up to you within the next hour for you and the girls. We offered them something when you first arrived, but they wanted to eat with you. Such sweethearts," he complimented before pumping sanitizer into his hands and smoothly ducking out of the room.

I couldn't believe that the stress of the last few weeks had landed me in the hospital. As soon as I got my voice back, I vowed to praise God for saving me and keeping me. I guess He wasn't through with me yet. He had to love me somehow, someway, because there was no reason I should be walking away with only a few bumps and bruises with all that had transpired.

I spent a total of three days in the hospital and was on my way to making a full recovery. I was excited to be getting out so I could continue my job search and get back on my feet once and for all. My girls were depending on me and I could no longer let them down. My breakthrough was coming—I just knew and felt it. All I had to do now was stay clear of any women who could be my ultimate downfall. I was truly changed.

As I dressed in my clothes to go home, I listened to sports highlights on the TV. The girls were knocked out on the couch. It was just after eight in the morning and the sun was peeking through the blinds. It looked and felt like today would be a beautiful and blessed day in more than one way.

A knock sounded at the door followed by a soft, "Jay?"

I paused from pulling my striped jogging pants up my legs. I knew that voice anywhere. It was not the nurse, a doctor, or anyone related to the hospital. As I made myself presentable and went to the door, my assumptions were proven correctly.

It was none other than my ex-wife.

"Jamaika. Hey." I'm sure she noticed the surprised look on my face and heard the excitement in my voice. "What are you doing here? How'd you, uh, know where I was?"

"Good morning," she said, twisting her fingers nervously. "One of your girls texted me a few days ago that you had a stroke. I no longer live in Illinois, but I drove back here to check on you and make sure you're okay."

"What?" I looked back at my girls who were still sleeping peacefully. It had to have been Summer. She was such a quick thinker. I chuckled, "How in the world did she even know your number, I wonder?"

"Probably my business card that I put in your book. She mentioned it was lying beside you where she found you," Jamaica concluded with a shrug, entering as I stepped back. She looked around and then back at me. "She said you guys are living in a...*hotel*, is it? What exactly is going on, Jay?"

"Gotta love the kids' honesty." I scratched my scalp and sat on the edge of the bed. "Yeah, it's all true. *Long* story."

"Well, you can explain it to me on your way back home. I didn't drive four hours not to figure out what's going on."

"You drove four hours? For...*me?*"

She said nothing more and instructed that I meet her downstairs in the black Cadillac truck that was parked outside.

"So where do you stay exactly?" I asked as Jamaika drove and I sat in the passenger seat of her luxury truck. Her vehicle smelled just like I remembered her—sweet and feminine, like a bed of jasmine flowers.

"Detroit is now our home. We moved over a year ago when Levi's firm expanded. But we still have a place in Illinois."

"Life has been good to you, I see. I'm happy for you." And I was *truly* was. She deserved it.

"Thank you. And yes, God has really shown Himself mighty to us." She was quiet for a few moments, tapping her thumbs on the steering wheel. "You are welcome to stay at our second home with your girls until you get back on your feet. Summer also told me you were fired, so I realize things have been hard on you."

"You can say that again. I'll be all right though."

"You don't look all right." She stole a peek in my direction. "Now, I know about the stroke and all the other misfortunes, but what happened to your face?"

Ashamed, I shook my head and wondered if I should tell the truth. I guess it was the least I could do. "It's the result of sleeping with a married woman who may be pregnant with my third child."

She shook her head as well, smirking. Her eyes never left the road. "Same ole womanizing Jay. When will you learn?"

"Wait a minute. I just realized what you said a while ago. I don't want you pitying me. Is this some sort of setup? Stay at YOUR house?" I questioned, looking at her out the corner of my eye.

"Yes, my second house with my husband," she said with nonchalance. "I'd rather someone stay there than us paying a mortgage and only visiting twice out of the year. It's just collecting dust."

I sat soundlessly for a few moments, taking it all in. "And what will your husband think of this? Does he even know you're here?"

She never answered. Instead, she continued driving to the hotel, where we gathered all of our belongings and checked out. After a lengthier drive up a few winding roads, we eventually pulled into the gated community of her second home. I hid my surprise as I admired everything.

Their home was far from ordinary. With two levels and a spacious layout, the house favored something right out of a movie. It had beautifully sculpted trees and bushes surrounding it, healthy flowers that were bloomed and brightly colored, and there was even a fountain out front that greeted everyone who pulled in. I could see that off to the side there was a pool, basketball court, and mini jungle gym. *This was living*, I thought.

We sat immobile as she ducked her head towards her phone, attempting to disable the alarm. I kept my mouth closed until she frowned and scratched her forehead in confusion.

"Need help?"

"No, this stupid thing is saying the Wi-Fi isn't connected. I was trying to turn off the security cameras."

"Turn them off or on?"

"Off," she clarified. "I don't want my husband logging in and seeing you here if he decides to randomly check. There are literally about 100 cameras around here."

I nodded my head, understanding. "Aaahh. So, he *doesn't* know you're doing this. Now are you SURE about this?"

"It's the least I can do as a Christian. It's not about our past or history together. If you weren't my ex-husband, I still would do it. And besides, despite all the stress and mess you put me through, you took care of home. So, I'd be remiss not to return the favor."

"Oh, and about that," I told her softly, reaching out to touch her arm, "I read your book and even though I knew what I did, I still didn't understand the magnitude of how much damage I caused and I'm sorry. Like...like the baby I caused you to miscarry. I had no idea. I feel like a monster...and...and...the 200 times that I..."

She held up her hand, not wanting me to go further. "You *were* a monster," she clarified.

I dropped my head. "It goes without saying, but I pray you've healed mentally, physically, and emotionally from the scars I inflicted, Jamaika. I mean that from the bottom of my heart."

She smiled tearfully. "I forgave you a long time ago, so there's no reason to even go through all this again. I'm happy...my life is complete; I now have a healthy marriage and family, and I love myself more than I ever have. The past is just that...the past."

I could accept that. We woke the girls up and moved our belongings into the house. She was not exaggerating; there was a camera in every room, with every angle imaginable. She explained how they had a break-in a few months back, so they had taken precaution.

I settled in one of the guestrooms and got the girls situated in a room down the hall. I could not thank Jamaika enough as she showed me where everything was, told me to utilize their monthly cleaning services if anything needed tidying, and even gave me directions to the nearest grocery stores and malls. What shocked me most was her handing me the keys to their winter truck that she said they hardly ever used because of gas mileage.

"Drive it SAFELY if you need to. I know you have a car, but it's perfect for when the weather's not so great. No speeding or getting tickets," she joked and then added, "Now we aren't due for another appearance until late September so that gives you a few months. Please EMAIL me when you're moving out or if you have any questions. I'll let our maid supervisor know you'll be here. Don't call. I don't want anything looking suspicious to Levi."

As she spoke, my eyes focused on her lips involuntarily. I just couldn't help it. She looked stunning, dressed in her dark grey bodysuit and matching fedora that was cocked atop her head. Large, turquoise feathered earrings and wedge sandals completed her look along with a sleek ponytail that touched her mid-back.

"Thank you. I really mean it. This was beyond helpful and generous of you..."

She shrugged as though it were no big deal and then clapped her hands once. "Well, I'm going to visit my parents and then be on my way back to Michigan. Take care, you hear? And please stay out of trouble for the sake of your girls. Seriously, Jalen. It's time out for the silly games and playing with people's hearts and lives."

"I hear you. I really do, Jamaika. Drive safely. Good looking out again."

She eased her purse unto her shoulder, and then sauntered to where the girls were still admiring their new living space and bade them a goodbye. Then, without another word or look back, she was gone and halfway down the road. I watched her taillights until they could no longer be seen. I missed what I had...and I honestly believe I was very much in love with my ex-wife still, but that was old news.

Chapter Six

(Three weeks later)

Jamaika

It had been almost a month since I did the unimaginable and allowed my ex-husband to stay in my second home. God truly must have been working in and through me to offer up such a deed. This was the same man who had caused me much stress and pain; this was the same guy who had raped me many times during our marriage; this was the same guy who stepped out on me with multiple women on multiple occasions throughout our 13 years together, causing me to have sexual diseases, insecurities, and trust issues, among other things.

Why did I care so much? Of course, any love for him had diminished long ago. Perhaps my concern was for the girls more than anything; no child, teenager, or even adult deserved to be homeless and living in unstable conditions. A piece of me—the God in me—also wanted to help out a fellow "brother" in Christ. This gesture was extensive, but I knew everything would work out. I expected Jalen to email me every day saying that he had a job offer but I had yet to hear from him regarding that matter.

The same night that I arrived back to Detroit, I had gotten my husband's phone and deleted the camera app off his phone. There was no telling when he might go randomly snooping to see what was going on back in Illinois. I should have been open and honest with him in the first place. I told my mom what I did, and although she was a bit disappointed that I wasn't upfront with my husband, she also understood that some things were better left unsaid.

I headed home to Levi now. The kids were at their summer school program and the babies were at daycare. We wanted just a few hours of alone time and had planned this day, weeks ago. I snuck and picked up a few pieces of new lingerie and planned to show my baby a good time. We did not have to be quiet. We did not have to close the door, nor did we have to look over our shoulders for peeking eyes as we made love. I grew excited thinking of all the possibilities and rare opportunities we had for the next six hours.

I tiptoed in the house and knew Levi was asleep. It was much too quiet. He normally had the surround sound system blasting in his den or a movie playing in our home theatre. I heard nothing as I walked through the house with my bags, calling, "Baby?"

Our Detroit home was a one-level, unlike our Illinois home, but it still was just as beautiful and well thought out. Levi had hired people to build it from the ground up with only a blueprint and a prayer. The only difference with this house was there was no basketball court outside. Levi thought it was a good idea to put a gym inside our home.

Sometimes I wondered why God saw fit to bless us so much financially and in other areas of our life. How did we get so fortunate? We had gorgeous and healthy children, several homes and cars, and multiple streams of income that kept us in the overflow. We were truly favored, and I was forever grateful.

I settled in my bedroom after giving up my search for Levi. I quickly showered, sprayed my favorite fragrance on my wrists, and then dressed in the satin and lace garments I'd picked up from the women's boutique. I slipped on a pair of red pumps and texted Levi to meet me in the bedroom. I waited with my legs crossed in the center of the oversized bed. I could hear him slowly making his way in, not long after.

I closed my eyes, arched my back, and then lowered my voice a few decibels, speaking, "Hey, Big Daddy."

I expected him to scoop me up and take me right then and there. I expected him to rain kisses down on my skimpily clad body. I expected him to make a sound of approval or do *something*. Instead, he wrapped his large hands around my ankles and pulled me so that I was on the edge of the bed and staring back at him.

"Let's watch a movie," he said simply.

"Baaaaaabe, really? We have the house all to ourselves and THIS is what you want to get into?"

He said nothing more, stripping down to his boxer-briefs and tossing the remainder of his clothes down on the floor. He joined me under the covers, pulling me close against him. As he began to show my body love with deep massages and sloppy wet kisses, I could sense that he was getting the movie going. With a few clicks of the remote, I knew he was getting us setup with something that would soon be watching us.

"Mmmm," I moaned slightly as his hand slipped under my gown.

"Baby, you're going to miss the good part," he whispered.

"*This* is the good part."

He chuckled against my flesh. "No, I'm

talking about the movie. Look. Look."

I was trying to figure out why he was so into this stupid movie but didn't question him. Reluctantly, I forced myself to leave euphoria and peek around his head to look at the TV screen. The movie was black and white, and the actor looked oddly familiar. If you ask me, the movie was boring because the actor only moved around in one room.

"What in the world?" I squinted my eyes as my husband stopped kissing my body completely and his hand left my breast to cup the back of my head as he forced me to look at the TV screen.

He sat up fully, gritting his teeth and mumbling, "See the movie? Looks interesting, right?"

My heart dropped in my chest. This wasn't a movie at all. This was video footage from the surveillance cameras at our Illinois home. I was watching Jalen move around in one of our guestrooms as he folded up some clothes. How in the world Levi had gotten into the deleted apps was a mystery to me but I knew I was in deep trouble.

His hands left the back of my head as he scooted to the edge of the bed. His eyes were fiery, and I was almost certain that there was steam leaving his ears. Okay, maybe that was an exaggeration, but he was *pissed*. "You want to explain why your ex-husband is in *our* house…where *I* pay bills? I mean, especially since I had no idea you guys were still in contact with each other. I'm trying to put the pieces together and I guess that explains why he came to your book signing. Is there something you want to tell me? Y'all messing around or something? TALK, Jamaika."

I swallowed the lump in my throat. Talking

was literally the last thing I could do. There were no words that would sound right, and truthfully, I didn't really want to explain anyway. I just wanted to hide or run far, far away. I had never seen Levi so angry, and I knew it was only going to get worse if I didn't start talking.

"Baby, calm down..." I rested a hand on his shoulder. "It's not what you think. You know I would never cheat on you!"

"I'm not calming down! Don't tell me how I should feel right now. It's clear you've lost your mind so I'm going to help you find it. Get off of me, Jamaika, and start talking. *Right* now."

His hand came up to rub his forehead but I figured he was ready to hit me, so I flinched, cowering backward. I guess it was a natural reaction, something that would have taken place years ago with Jalen. His eyes softened slightly.

"I'm not going to hit you, nor would I *ever* hit you, and you KNOW that. But I seriously could shake you real hard right now." He gritted his teeth and made a choking motion with his hands. "Why did you think this was a good idea, Jamaika?"

"I wanted to make sure he had a home for his girls."

"That's all fine, but why didn't you come to ME first? We're supposed to talk these things out. Imagine my surprise getting an email saying I've unsubscribed from our security alerts when I know I didn't. When I went to download it again, I discovered the passwords were changed. Then when I called to get a report of everything, I'm told we've had more activity than usual in the last few weeks than the entire year. What is going on, Jamaika?"

I sat up on the bed completely, knowing I had to be 100 percent honest. My husband deserved a proper explanation, no matter how uncomfortable this conversation would be. I nervously explained how Jalen had a stroke and one of his daughters called me; I told him how they had nothing and needed a place to stay and a car to get from point A to point B, so I offered up our spare home and car.

Levi paced with his hands on his hips, stopping only to glare at me. "And the book signing?"

"Baby, I had no clue he was coming or even knew about me writing a book. Remember we sent out flyers all over the Midwest. Maybe he came across a flyer and popped up. That was the first time I had seen him in years. I swear!"

"Don't swear." Levi looked unimpressed with my explanation, but he knew it was the truth. I NEVER lied to my husband. "Why didn't you come to me first?"

"I knew you wouldn't approve."

"And you're absolutely right. I can appreciate you wanting to help. That's just the kind of person you are, and I realize that, baby, but this man almost destroyed you. When I met you, you were BROKEN...because of *his* actions. I've forgiven him too, but I have a major problem with him. I'm not okay with this."

"I'll do whatever you want me to do, baby. I'm sorry! I know I should've told you from the jump." I reached for his hand.

"If he didn't have kids, I'd tell you to give him one week. But I'm not going to take away shelter for his girls. He can stay until the end of August and the house better be clean and the same way we left it when we go back in September," he explained firmly. "Do I make myself clear?"

"Yes, baby. I understand," I whispered as a

single tear rolled down my face. "Please don't be mad at me."

"I'm far from. Come here."

He caught my tear with his thumb. We kissed each other as if we hadn't seen each other in months. I could recall this was the first time I had ever been dishonest with my husband and it would surely be my last. In the morning, I planned to send Jalen a long email and relay Levi's message to him. But for now, I needed to make up for my mess-ups. The mood that I thought was ruined was quickly ignited and I was soon mounting my husband's waist as I cried out his name unapologetically.

Chapter Seven

Jalen

Jay,

I hope this email finds you well. This serves as a notice that my husband knows about you staying in our home. He was not too happy about it, but I explained everything. He does not mind you staying until we return, but please make sure the house is exactly how you left it.

Make sure to email me when you find a job. How is that going anyway? I know our neighbors, the Johnsons (black and white house up the road), are always hiring people at their family-owned grocery store in North Waukegan. It's not the most glamorous job, but they pay well, and treat their employees with respect. Our oldest son sweeps there for a few bucks whenever we're in town. He LOVES them.

More than anything, from what you told me, trouble seems to follow you and you're experiencing trial after trial. I think it's time you've forgiven yourself for all the things you've done. It's time to get your life together once and for all. Levi's old church is small and intimate (off of 108th and Apple Blossom Road) but I'm sure no one knows who you are. You should go there one day and rededicate your life back to God. It's *time out for all of your old habits. You can't go back and change what you used to do, but you CAN start over! Focus on the Creator and NOT what your mess created.*

Tell me how it works out for you. Take care.

-Jamaika

I scrolled over the email again and again, feeling the sincerity and concern seeping from my ex-wife's words. It made my heart do a backflip that she cared so much. But she was also right. I needed God in my life, and not just for a prayer when things went wrong. I needed God on my good days. I needed God when I was content. I needed God when I was sick. I needed God when I was fathering Summer and Autumn and facing challenges. I needed God *period*. Without Him, life was not going to make sense or get any better—as a former pastor, I knew that firsthand. It was something I once preached to the masses.

Sunday was in two days, so I planned to attend the church with the girls. They probably had not been in a church setting since they were little and lived with me. It was time that we all became more acquainted with God. I had to be the man of the house and lead them in a purpose-filled life. Right now, it was sort of hard to do when I didn't even have a home to lead them in. But I knew the God I served had already forgiven me and wanted to bless me; it was just a matter of me not turning back to my wicked ways.

I cooked breakfast for the girls with a light heart and explained to them how we would be changing up some things really soon.

"Did your mom ever take you to church?"

Autumn shook her head, biting into her forkful of eggs. "Only around the holidays. You know, Easter, Mother's Day, and Christmas."

I nodded. "Well, we'll be starting a new tradition. We've gotta get back to Eden."

"What does that mean?" Summer questioned before sipping on her glass of pulp-free orange juice.

"I haven't been the best father then or now. When you girls were little, I did a lot of women wrong, including Jamaika. I did your mother wrong. I made so many mistakes, but I would have a fit if you dated a guy like me and he did you the same way. So, starting today, I'm starting over fresh, but I need your help. I need us all to make an effort to do better. Whether it's having a better attitude about things we can't change, praying more, or just showing love to each other more. We've got to start small and allow God to do the rest."

They listened carefully and seemed to understand where I was coming from. Autumn looked up from buttering her toast. "So, is that why Mom left us, because you did her wrong?"

I thought about that for a moment. "I won't say that. I guess you girls are old enough to understand. Your mom got married in another country. She hasn't returned any of my calls or texts, and she's blocked me from any of her social media profiles, so for now, we're all we got. We'll give her time and pray for her, but I know Rochelle wouldn't just leave you two to fend for yourself.

Maybe she wanted me to really develop a relationship with you girls before returning. Who knows? But instead of passing judgments or making assumptions, we're just going to pray for her. Understand?"

They nodded in silence, looking from me to each other in surprise.

"But that's enough of that talk. I have enough left from my check for us to get *one* church outfit a piece. Let's say we do a little shopping?"

That seemed to brighten their spirits. I smirked as we headed out a half-hour later and headed to the same mall where Jamaika had her book signing. It was a mall we all loved. We shopped together and surprisingly they didn't cringe when I helped them pick out appropriate skirts and dresses. In return, they helped me pick out the perfect suit jacket to go with a shirt I already had.

We walked around for an hour and window-shopped more than we physically shopped, but it was okay. As long as we were out of the house and spending time together, that was *most* important. As I reached my spending limit, I decided it was time to leave. We headed for the exit doors, and I dropped my head briefly to look at my cell phone. Any day now it would be turned off. I had not paid my bill in over 12 days, but I was still able to access the Internet and send text messages. I looked back up and nearly pummeled into a woman who toted various bags.

"Oh, excuse me."

"*Jalen?*"

I whipped my head back around. I rolled my eyes as I realized who was speaking to me. "I have nothing to say to you, and if you don't mind, I'm trying to spend the afternoon with my girls."

"Stop that. Let's talk. Please," Marisha begged, reaching for my arm. She looked much different than when I had previously seen her. She tugged on my arm until I followed her to a bench. "It's not what you think."

"I figured you would say that," I told her and then called out for the girls. They were walking ahead, giggling and talking. I handed over a 20-dollar bill to Summer. "Go to the food court and buy ONE dessert you two can share. I want my change too."

They giggled and walked off.

I turned back to Marisha, licking my parched lips. When she did not speak right away, I lifted my eyebrows in irritation. "Well? I'm waiting."

Marisha sighed heavily and smoothed her hair back in nervousness. "Listen, I lied about a majority of what I told you."

I nodded. That was obvious.

"I *am* from the West Indies, but I was raised in America from the time that I was four years old. I've lived in Waukegan for 12 years, and I work at the firm where you were interviewing. I did some modeling as a teenager, and I *do* sell my photography online, but I'm in no way trying to make a career out of it like I told you."

I shook my head. "Why lie?"

"I did not tell you the truth because I knew it would be a lot for you to handle."

"What would be a lot for me to handle? We were just getting to know each other. It wasn't like I was going to marry you based off of our first conversation."

"I understand that, but my life is very complex. I was afraid you would be turned off and

78

never talk to me again, so I…indulged, I guess you could say."

"So that's why you stopped calling and had someone answer your phone and act like you weren't there? I felt like we were in high school again. That wasn't cool at all. You could have just told me you weren't interested."

"Oh, but I was…and I still am. I really, *really* like you, Jalen," Marisha confessed, placing her bags down on the ground. "Can we talk somewhere else? Can we go back to your place?"

"I have my girls with me, as you've seen, so right now it's a…"

"I have my children with me too," she interrupted, standing up. "They're running around here somewhere."

"*Children?*" I repeated. The last I remembered, she had no husband or children.

"Yes, that's just what we need to talk about. Maybe we can just sit in the food court then? But I can't go another day without coming clean to you. When I saw you at the office last month, my heart stopped. I was sure that I would never see you again."

Reluctantly, I agreed to meet her in the food court. She walked off to find her children while I looked for my girls. They were still in line when I rounded the corner, so I found a seat and then waved them over. Marisha made her way over as I put our bags down. There were not one, or two, but *three* preteen girls walking behind her. They all favored Marisha and were good looking with naturally curly hair, smooth, dark skin, and piercing hazel eyes. They were a sight to behold.

"Jalen, please meet Sabrina, Amaya, and Amina…these are my girls."

I nodded at the girls, waving. "Nice to meet you. Marisha, these are my twins, Summer and Autumn. I see we had a common theme of naming our kids with Ss and As."

Everyone smiled and waved shyly, and then Marisha scooted in closer to me. Our daughters sat at another table, making small talk while they ate.

"So, what's up? We've established that you lied about having children. What's next? You're married too?"

"*Was,*" Marisha clarified softly, looking down at her hands. "He died overseas, three years ago, in Kabul."

"Are you serious?"

"*Very.* He left me and my girls to fend for ourselves, but he died a hero. He didn't die in battle, but he stayed with one of his injured comrades until help came. As the medics arrived, a suicide bomber drove through and set off an explosion, killing them all," she explained, keeping her voice down.

"The girls have no idea how their father died. I couldn't spare them the details. They just assumed war meant death, and when he never came home, they knew what happened. We couldn't even bury him or give him a proper funeral. What was left of his remains, we cremated," she added softly.

A chill ran down my spine. I was still confused as to why she was so secretive and dishonest to begin with. I would have still thought she was attractive and interesting; I would have accepted her truth regardless of her marital status and the fact that she was the mother of three. It made her even more beautiful and admirable, in my eyes.

"And the guy that answered your phone that day?"

"Yeah…about that," she said with disappointment. "So, as you know from our run-in last month, I work for your ex-mistress's husband. When he found out we were talking, he warned me about you and told me not to get involved because you were bad news. I happened to be at work when you called and he answered, pretending that I wasn't there. I know, I know…it's all a big mess, and I take full responsibility for it. I'm so sorry. If we could meet all over again, I would make it happen in a heartbeat."

I did not know what to think or believe anymore. It just all seemed so strange and unnecessary that things went down this way, but one fact remained. I still liked Marisha. I wasn't trying to marry the girl, or even seriously date her, but I did not mind getting to know her better—the REAL her. She looked like she was trying to make it on her own and make sense of everything, just like me. There was no harm in being her friend. I remembered Jamaika's advice to take it slowly from here on out and focus on God. I stood up from the table, walked away a few feet, and then walked back with an outstretched hand. Marisha and the kids looked on in confusion.

"Hello, beautiful. I could not help noticing that you were alone at this table. My name is Jalen Owens. I'm divorced, and I'm a single parent to twin teenage daughters who are my world. I'm not looking for love, but I'd like to establish a friendship with you and see where God takes us, if you'll have me."

Marisha chuckled behind the hand that covered her mouth. She blushed a little and then bit her bottom lip. There were tears of relief in her eyes when she spoke, "Hello, Jalen, I'm Marisha Blackman. I am widowed with three daughters. I also am not looking for love but would appreciate your companionship, as I navigate life as a single parent. It's nice to meet you."

I shook her hand and then kissed the back of it.

"People must think we're crazy from afar," she added, still giggling.

"Who cares what they think?" I returned her smile and then looked over at the girls. "Why don't we plan another outing some other time? I'm without employment momentarily, but even if we do something free just to talk, that'd be great."

"Yes, I'd like that a lot," Marisha agreed and patted my hand. "Thank you for listening and understanding…and forgiving."

"Thank you for being open and honest with me."

We hugged and parted ways.

Chapter Eight

Sunday morning rolled around, and it would be the first time I stepped in a church since the incident with the underage worship leader. I was nervous for whatever reason, but excited as well. It felt good to be on my way to worship and give God glory. In spite of the chaos lately, I was thankful and glad. Things could be a lot worse. The girls and I got up extra early and dressed in our brand new "church clothes." We ate breakfast over small talk. I emailed Jamaika and told her we were giving her husband's old church a try. I did not stick around for a reply because it was time to head out.

We rode to the church with the upbeat melodies of Kirk Franklin floating throughout the truck. I had even reached out to Marisha and encouraged her to come along with me, though I doubted she would attend. Although she believed in God, she did not seem like the churchgoing type, but I could be wrong. We arrived at the quaint house of worship and there was quite a bit of cars already parked outside. I wondered if some sort of guest speaker would be there or if they were hosting a revival. Either way, I knew the Lord would have a Rehoboth Word for the girls and I.

We settled in the back of the church on the last pew. The church was tiny from the outside, yet it appeared more spacious as people piled in row by row. I was glad we arrived when we did because before long, there were no more empty seats. I had missed this scene. Mothers wore large church hats, children fidgeted with their uncomfortable attire and stared at the people behind them, and the choir rocked back and forth with matching robes while they sang. There was truly nothing like a good ole Church of God in Christ service.

My girls looked on in curiosity, taking it all in. I vowed right then and there that churchgoing would be a regular occurrence for them. They had to know Jesus for themselves, and I would do everything in my power to give them that opportunity. Service was starting soon, and I was even more eager as the congregation roared with admiration at the man of God that came out from the side. He looked "blessed and highly favored," as the church folks said. He was dressed like one of the preachers you would see broadcasted on TV and spoke with authority as he waved and made his presence known. I wondered who he was.

The choir sang all of my favorite songs. Before worship was even over, I had a face full of tears and my knees were wobbly. The Holy Spirit was definitely in the building and I could not fully stand in His presence. I lifted my hands to the ceiling and tried to see past the tears, but all I saw was a hand motioning me forward. I told the girls to stay put as I was summoned to the nearly full altar by the guest pastor. He stared me directly in the eyes with a hint of compassion behind his dark eyes. With the help of a male usher, I was escorted to a row of pillows near the altar and knelt down. I buried my face in my hands and soon felt another hand against my forehead.

"Son, you're tired. I see it on your face; I see it in the way you carry yourself, and I feel it in your spirit. You're literally tired from running from God and the call on your life," the nameless minister spoke closely to my ear. "You and I both know what God is saying in this moment."

I nodded and kept quiet. God had definitely revealed a few things in my spirit this week, and Jamaika had confirmed them. I needed to get back right with God before it was too late.

"While you still have breath in your body, it's time you allow God into your heart and life once and for all. You can't keep running, son. Nothing will work out for you. No job, no relationship, no endeavor under the sun. If God isn't the head of your life, what exactly do you have?"

"I have nothing without God. I *am* nothing without God," I cried.

He cupped both hands around my head, as I finally looked him in the eye. "I know who you are; I recognized you the moment you stepped in our church. I know life has been tough for you. It's not easy for anyone to go from one extreme to the next. You were one of the biggest public figures in Illinois until the scandals and secrets came out. But that does not mean God has taken away your purpose. There is still an unfinished assignment that you must complete. You've brought many souls to Christ in spite of your sin, and there is still a great reward for you in Heaven, but you must accept God again in your life. You can't do this on your own, Jalen. Trust me, I know. I was in your same shoes 18 years ago, but God saved me and delivered me."

I held onto the pastor tightly and cried openly. I was sure he had my snot and tears on his shoulder, but at this point, my soul was more important than a $300 suit. We hugged for some time as he patted my back and prayed over me.

"So, what's it going to be, my brother? Today is the day. God is saying NOW is the time! Are you going to stop running?"

I nodded, still unable to form words through my tears.

"Repeat after me. Dear Lord, I admit that I am a sinner. I have done many things that don't please You. I have lived my life for myself only. I am sorry, and I repent. I ask You to forgive me. I believe that You died on the cross for me, to save me. You did what I could not do for myself. I come to You now and ask You to take control of my life; I surrender and give it to You. From this day forward, help me to live every day for You and in a way that is pleasing in Your sight. I love You, Lord, and I thank You because my name is now written in the Lamb's Book of Life. Amen."

I repeated after the pastor and completed my prayer of salvation. By the time I was done, my daughters were at my side, crying and wanting to give their lives to God as well. The church seemed to burst into corporate praise as they saw my girls willing to surrender to God at such a young age. The pastor called up two female youth pastors and directed them to Summer and Autumn. It caused me to smile proudly and cry harder. This was turning out to be one of my favorite days by far.

At the end of service and after a life-changing word, I was drained but in a good way. I had cried all the tears I could muster up, and the girls could not stop talking about how much they were excited about their "new lives." I decided that I would treat them to dinner at a fancy restaurant, even though my bank account really could not handle that right now. As we made our way to the exit, a hand reached out and grabbed onto my arm.

"Hey, Jalen. I was hoping to catch you before you left."

I turned back and looked at the pastor who

had prayed over me earlier. "Oh, hi, how are you? Thank you again for that awesome prayer and Word today."

"You know, I come here once a month. I'm the presiding bishop over this church, so I know every member fairly well. It was amazing last week to see your face in the spirit, and then officially meet you today. I am also a friend of Jamaika and Levi's, who is also my Godson. From my understanding, she told you to attend the church. Is that correct?"

I nodded. "Yes, she did, sir."

"Well, it certainly pays to be obedient." He winked and extended his hand. We shook hands and hugged briefly. "If you need anything—a prayer, references, or simply a friend to talk to, call me. You and your girls take care. I'll be back next month, and I hope to see you then."

"You too, man. I appreciate you. God bless."

As he walked off, I nodded for the girls to follow me outside. They grabbed hands and raced to the car, something they always did. With a smile, I lagged behind and looked down at what the pastor handed me. It was five crisp 100-dollar bills wrapped around three business cards. One business card held the pastor's information. Another business card was an owner of a realty company, and the third was the information for a job recruitment company. My heart burst with gladness. Not only had I been blessed with money, but also resources to get a job and a place to live.

I stopped in my tracks, looked up towards the Heavens, and pointed my finger. "Thank You, God! Thank You!"

As promised, I took the girls out for a fancy dinner date and we talked about what life would look like from here on out. I promised to be their provider, biggest supporter, and the leader God intended me to be.

"Daddy wasn't always the greatest example, but starting today, I'm going to do a whole lot better. You hear me?"

They nodded.

"I love you, girls."

"We love you too, Dad," they said in unison.

Chapter Nine

"Mr. Owens, I'm glad you called and setup an interview. I've heard great things about you."

I entered the office where a slender black man sat on the edge of a conference table. He had on a pair of thick, bifocal glasses and his eyes appeared slightly larger than what they probably were. He donned a dark blue suit and slacks, and stood to about 5'7" as he greeted me with a hug.

"Welcome, welcome. Have a seat," he added with a warm smile.

"Thank you. Nice to meet you officially," I told him sincerely.

It was exactly three days since I had rededicated my life to God, two days since calling the number on the business card, and one day since I had completed two separate phone interviews with the man standing before me. It did not take long for God to move at all, and I was 99 percent sure that the job was already mine. I had one more step in the hiring process before I could give my daughters the long-awaited news.

Cornell Stacey, the guy who stood before me, owned the company and was looking for a senior recruiter. The job was simple; I literally just had to call qualified individuals and interview them. With every new hire, I would receive a bonus on top of my salary.

"So, Mr. Owens, when can you start?" Cornell asked, wasting no time at all. "I like you and I like your spirit. I think you'll be a great addition to the company."

"Immediately," I answered quickly. "I can start right away, sir."

He smiled. "I was hoping you said that. We have a corner office waiting for you as we speak. Follow me."

Shocked at how quickly things were happening, I followed behind him as he led me down a long hallway, through several double doors, and then to an office surrounded completely by glass. The office took my breath away. In addition to a large desk, I had a loveseat, an area rug with the company logo on it, and a mini fridge. There was a mounted TV in the corner of the office and all of the latest gadgets were available at my fingertips. The office overlooked the company commons, which featured a daycare, fitness center, and cafeteria. I could also see miles and miles of well-manicured trees, bushes, and flowerbeds.

I loved the company already and hadn't even started. I turned back to Cornell who was watching me like a proud father. "Wow, this is incredible," I told him.

He showed me around a couple other places, introduced me to a few people on the floor, and then told me to have a good rest of the day since I would be starting first thing in the morning. I wanted to do a backflip; that's how excited I was. Instead, I thanked him once more and gave a half-hug.

"You're very welcome. Send my love to Jamaika and Levi, will you? They told me you were a phenomenal worker and would be perfect for the company."

I stood in silence for a moment. My heart fluttered at the thought that they had vouched for me. I had brought so much turmoil to their lives and yet they were now looking out for *me*. It touched me deeply to know I was not only forgiven by God but by the people I hurt the most.

"Will do," I said, offering a final goodbye. I headed home to tell the girls the good news and write Jamaika a thank you email.

I sat down to write it with a light heart. I no longer would have to rely on handouts from the government just to keep my head above water. God had answered all of my prayers, and I knew I would be able to truly provide for my girls once the money started rolling in.

Jamaika & Levi,

Words can't describe how elated I am right now! I rededicated my life to God on Sunday, received several blessings that same day, and today, I landed a job with Cornell Stacey (he sends his love). Thank you for referring me and looking out for me. That's the TRUE definition of grace and mercy.

I will be able to move out of your home soon, and again, I thank you so much for allowing me to stay here while I figure things out. I pray God continues to bless you two and I'll be sure to "pay it forward."

I'll email you both when I have secured an apartment.

-J.O.

I sent the email, closed the computer, and then checked my phone. I had several text messages from Marisha, who was checking on me and asking if I needed help finding a job. I happily text back that I had landed one just this afternoon. She also wanted to meet up and talk, no strings attached. She had a lot on her mind, and she was in need of a good laugh. I agreed to meet up with her at the park. That way, our daughters could do a little bonding as well.

I felt sorry for Summer and Autumn; school wasn't starting up for another month and they had not really had much of a summer. On top of that, they would be attending a brand-new school in a new city, so life was completely different now for them. I vowed to do my best to accommodate them.

We pulled up to the park and Marisha was leaning against her car with a stressed look upon her face. I told Summer and Autumn to go on and enjoy the elements, while I slowly approached her with my hands in my pocket. It was a beautiful day out, the sun was shining, and the breeze was just right. But the look on her face was alarming, causing a bit of a dark cloud to hang over our heads.

"What's going on? Everything okay?"

She nodded, running her fingers through her hair. "I'm fine. The girls just needed a breather. *I* needed a breather. I can't wait for them to head back to school next month."

I chuckled, looking over in amusement. "It's that bad, huh?"

"Yes. *That* bad," she laughed. "There's so much estrogen, bad attitudes, and cosmetics in the house I could scream! You're a man. How do *you* do it?"

"My girls aren't really into cosmetics just yet and I don't think either of them have started their menstrual cycles." I shuddered for effect. "But when that time comes, I plan to pray every day until they're married and out of the house."

We both laughed.

"Is their mother out of the picture, if you don't mind me asking?"

"Yeah. We were previously together, years ago, but she left them with me and started another life in another country without any warning or goodbyes."

"Oh, wow. What kind of mother would just leave her children like that?"

I shrugged and leaned against her car, looking at the girls all push each other on the swings. They were older, but still found it amusing to go as high and as fast as they could without falling off.

"I stopped wondering that and just figured I would enjoy my daughters and make their lives as simple as possible. I am not the perfect father and never was, so I can't judge anyone for any decision. But whether she comes back in their lives or not, I know God's got me and I've got them."

"That's a beautiful philosophy. You always seem so calm. How do you always have it all together?"

"Trust me. A couple weeks ago…heck, last week, I had thoughts of blowing my own head off. *Seriously*. It's always been the peace of God that keeps me going, even when I didn't recognize it. That's all I can say."

"I've never actually been to church as an adult, is that bad? Like, will I go to hell if I don't go to church?"

"*Going* to a physical church and *being* the church are two different things. No. God won't send you to hell because you didn't attend, but there will be judgement if you never accept Him or believe in Him. What matters most is the relationship between you and God. Do you at least believe in God, or are you one of those people who uses His name in vain?" I teased her during that last part, but I was genuinely curious.

"No, I'm very familiar with His signs and wonders. I believe in spirits, fate, God's timing, and all that good stuff. But I hate church. I hate everything it stands for."

"How so?"

"Just look around. You hear about all the fake pastors, the corruption and adulterous men, the judgmental church mothers, the bisexual worship leaders, and everything in between. The church is just like the world. I've never been to a church that was really about the people, even as a little girl. I grew up with parents who were churchgoers and they spent most of their time at church. As a result, they neglected home and quality time with their children, but that's a different story for a different day."

I swallowed hard at the first half of her statement. She would be turned off if she knew I was one of those "fake" pastors once upon a time. But that was all in the past and I had been redeemed in more ways than one. There was no reason for me to even feel guilty or ashamed anymore.

"Yeah, well, no church is perfect. That's a huge misconception. *Every* church is flawed in some way, just like there is no perfect person. Only Jesus was without flaw. But you shouldn't take past experiences or misconceptions and let that rob you of developing a solid relationship with God. I'm sure there is a church out there for you."

"We'll see about that, Jalen. We shall see. Maybe I'll take you up on the offer to come to church with you someday."

"Feel free. I went for the first time to my new church last week, and I'm already planning on joining this coming Sunday. My heart tells me that this is the place for me."

"That's awesome. I'm happy for you," she said and clapped her hands. "Well, I better get going. You've got your brand new job tomorrow and I've got some things to handle first thing in the morning. Thank you for chatting with me."

"My pleasure." I gave her a brief hug and kissed her cheek. "Take care, you hear?"

"You too."

Chapter Ten

The next morning, around 7:30, I pulled into the parking lot of my brand new job, *Stacey & Associates*. I had left out extra early to grab a special cup of coffee from the café not far from the house. I wasn't a big coffee drinker, but I figured it would come in handy for the productive day I would have.

As though I were some young, eager intern, I took the stairs instead of the elevator, and soon knocked on Cordell's office door.

He waved me in. "Good morning, Mr. Owens. How are you?"

"I'm doing really well. Excited to start this day."

"Well, we're certainly happy to have you. Once you're all settled in, page my office on extension 1-9-6-3, and I'll give you a rundown of today's tasks, but I trust that you'll get acquainted with everything very quickly. The previous recruiter left after only five weeks, so if we can keep you longer, that'd be an accomplishment."

I did as told and settled in my office that was already unlocked with air conditioning wafting throughout the 10 by 15-foot room. A basket of goodies awaited me filled with peanuts, peppermints, and other snacks that would satisfy my midday appetite since I forgot my lunch at home. I smiled at the gesture and sat my coffee cup down on the desk. I hung up my belongings in the closet and logged onto the computer. Then I paged Cordell who explained how to setup all my passwords and usernames for the company software.

He mentioned that I would not be starting interviews for another couple weeks, but he was going to send me an assistant in the meantime to train me. That was fine with me; I had no problem starting from the bottom and working my way up. I waited patiently as the assistant was called up and made a mental note to bring some pictures of my daughters to make the office feel a little bit more like home.

Through the glass, I saw a figure walk past once and then circle back around. I looked up, smiling at the woman who was now waving. Eventually, she motioned as if to ask if she could enter. I nodded and waved her in.

"Good morning, Mr. Owens," she sang, stepping inside. She wore a red dress that was much too tight for the workplace, in my opinion. On her feet were red-bottomed heels, and a gold belt that hugged her waist so snugly that I wondered if she could breathe. Her hair was curly and pulled off to one side of her head and cascaded down the other shoulder. "I'm your assistant slash trainer for the next two weeks. How are you? Welcome to the company."

I swallowed hard, trying not to look at her body and just focus on her face. She was gorgeous in every sense of the word and there was lust in her eyes. Everything about her screamed *temptation*. I prayed that satan would get thee behind, and then stood up to shake her hand. It was extra soft.

"I'm Jalen. Nice to meet you, uh…?"

"Oh! I'm sorry. I'm Randi. Randi Stacey." She leaned forward to adjust her stockings and her breasts nearly fell out of her bra. This had to be some sort of joke, or maybe it was a test. It was the first day on my new job and I was already trying to keep my mind from wandering down forbidden pastures. "Excuse me."

I continued to look away as she handled her business. I stuffed my hands in my pockets and whistled uncomfortably.

"Alright, I'm all set. So just a little bit about me," she began, rubbing her full lips together. "I've been with the company for six years. I'm the Assistant Vice President and Cordell's eldest daughter. I typically help train all of the new hires."

I felt a little bit better that she was my boss's daughter. "Nice."

"You look so tense. What's wrong?" she questioned with a smile and patted my arm. "Do I make you nervous?"

"Not at all. Just thinking about my girlfriend. She has a few pairs of red bottoms as well," I lied, hoping the mention of a girlfriend would deter her from flirting or crossing the line.

"Oh, these?" She bent her leg upward and rubbed a hand down the length of her calf. "They're super comfortable. I'm sure your girl likes the feel of them, like I do."

"Yeah. So anyway, what's up with the training?" I cut her off before she said or did anything else tastelessly. "When can we start?"

"Have a seat. Have a seat. We can go ahead and get started now, honey," she instructed.

I sat down, imagining that she would pull up a chair but instead she leaned on the back of my chair and reached around me as she pointed out the different functions of the computer. She was so close that I could feel her breath and feel each time she brushed her breasts against my shoulders or head. I looked out beyond the glass helplessly, knowing it would not look good if anyone passed by. I began to sweat with anxiety and panic.

"Would you like a chair to sit in?"

"No, no. I'm used to standing. I'm fine," she insisted and caught my eyes in the reflection of computer monitor. "Ever since I saw your name on the roster, I've been meaning to ask you something."

Oh, boy. Here we go…

"What's that?"

Randi lowered her voice, looking at the door, and then down at me. "Are you the same pastor that had all that scandalous stuff going on some odd years ago in Arlington Heights?"

That was the *last* discussion I wanted to have with her or anyone else. Still, I nodded anyway. "Um. Yeah, that's…uh, me unfortunately."

"I knew it!" She clapped in triumph. "Me and a coworker were debating if you were the same guy or not."

I closed my eyes briefly in disbelief, and then drummed my fingers along the keyboard. "You're correct, but I'd rather not talk to you or anyone else about this, please."

"I promise you're okay. I won't tell anybody," she cooed, rubbing my shoulder.

"I'm a completely different person now," I added. "I've changed my life and I've changed my ways, so you don't have to…"

Randi shook her head, giving me a reassuring look. "No, no. There's no need to be ashamed. I've followed you for years and I've always thought you were incredibly sexy. Honestly, if I were one of the women you were with, I would have never come forward. How childish is that? I mean, what we do in the bedroom is between us and…"

"Hey, hey. That's enough!" I spoke up, pushing away from the desk so that she was no

99

longer beside me. I stood up and backtracked to the door. "That's enough, okay? I think this kind of talk is pretty inappropriate for work. We've established that you knew me from my past, but if you don't mind, I'd like to keep it that way—in the past. I'm not the same man, nor am I interested in pursuing anything with you, so I'd appreciate it if you kept your comments and gestures to yourself."

Randi looked offended, hurt, and angry all at the same time. She held a hand over her chest and was quiet for a moment. Then she blew out a short breath, threw her hands up, and stormed out of the office. Her heels made a soft thud along the carpet. I watched her walk away until she could no longer be seen. Only then did I sigh and make my way back to my desk. I sat down with a huff. Now who was going to train me? How would I explain this to Cordell without throwing his daughter under the bus?

I figured I would play around on the computer and figure out a few things on my own until someone else came in to check on me. When lunchtime rolled around, I checked out the remainder of the office building and walked around. I headed to the cafeteria to grab an energy drink, and then sat down on a bench to enjoy the breeze.

As I sipped the energy drink slowly, I noticed a group of police officers heading up the sidewalk briskly. They looked like they were searching for something or *someone*, rather. I crossed my legs at the ankle, noticing that at the front of the group was Cordell. I wondered what was going on since it seemed like such a peaceful day. When he saw me, he pointed and walked a little bit faster. I waved slightly in confusion, squinting my eyes.

"There he is!" I heard someone say. I noticed Randi was at the back of the group, trying to keep up in her high heels. She looked distraught and her eyes were already piercing into mine. "That's him, officers."

I stood up, swallowing the lump in my throat. I had a feeling that something bad was about to occur but tried to remain calm until I had all the answers. "Is something wrong? What's going on?"

One of the officers looked from me to Randi, and then back again. "Ms. Stacey, are you *sure* this is the man who was watching child pornography on the screen?"

"I'm positive," she said, crossing her arms under her breasts.

"WHAT?" I spit out the little bit of energy drink I had sipped on and backed away as the police officers stepped forward. I saw handcuffs, angry faces, disappointed expressions, and a look of satisfaction on Randi's face in particular. She had set me up, and now all of the wrongs I had tried so hard to correct were crashing down all around me.

"She's lying! I would never do that! I have children of my own, but beyond that, why would I be watching something as SICK as child pornography? Please. You've got to believe me!" I held my palms out, trying not to resist too much but knowing I also had rights.

"That's exactly the problem! I believed people when they said to hire you, and clearly, that was a mistake. A man with your past shouldn't be working anywhere in this town *ever* again! You have issues and need HELP!" Cordell spat, nearly foaming at the mouth. "You're FIRED, you hear me? FIRED! Get him out of here, fellas!"

"On the ground…now!" the officers demanded in unison, surrounding me, and forcing me down.

They obviously had the wrong guy, but it was her word against mine, and how could I possibly be trusted? As Cordell accused, a man with my past should have left well enough alone and gotten a job someplace else.

Cordell stood off to the side, hugging Randi against him. She pretended to cry against his shoulder, while I stared at her with venom in my eyes. She had raised hell, all because I wasn't interested in her advances. Wow. I had no idea how I would get out of this situation, but my faith had to make way for a miracle. It was all I had at that point.

As I was pushed and pulled, yelled at, and looked down upon with disgust, all I could recite under my breath was, *"Though I walk through the valley of the shadow of death, I fear no evil, for You are with me. Your rod and Your staff, they comfort me. You prepare a table before me in the presence of my enemies; You have anointed my head with oil. My cup overflows…"*

"Oh, now he wants to go to scripture," one of the officers chuckled. "Figures. *They* always call on God after *they've* broken the law. Don't forget to call on Him when you get to the jail cell."

I ignored the chastising and continued to recite the renowned scripture again and again. I was now on the ground with bloodied and bruised wrists. They had even bound my ankles together. I sat in a fetal position, praying and hoping for the best. They gathered a statement from Randi and Cordell, and then asked me a few vague questions that had nothing to do with what she accused me of doing. No one wrote down any of my responses though, I noted.

"God, why You have forsaken me?" I whispered, defeated.

After the police officers wrapped up their botched interrogation and gathered everyone's contact information, they leaned to pick me up by the arms. There was a police officer on either side of me, literally carrying me since my feet and wrists were restricted. I felt like an animal and knew my wrists would be sore for days to come. My shoes were strewn about, and I tried to tell the hefty men, but no one listened to my pleas. They left my belongings on the bench and did not even bother to gently place me in the car. I hit my head in the process of getting in and could feel blood trickling down the right side of my face. I was sure that I had peed a little in my pants from all the roughhousing as well.

I thought about my daughters and the church I planned to join. I thought about my new job that had gone down the drain just as quickly as I had gotten it. Once again, even when trying to do right, somehow everything seemed to go left. Money for a lawyer was out of the question as everyone who was once close to me had grown sick of my mess-ups and letdowns. I didn't have much of anything and certainly couldn't pay for any legal expenses or representation. Who would pay my bail? Who would watch my girls? Would my one phone call privilege go to Jamaika so she could *again* come to my rescue and take the girls until I was released? Would I *ever* be released? Child pornography was a SERIOUS offense across the board, so freedom looked miles and miles away.

With the chatter of the overzealous police officers in my ears and the faint sounds of a dispatcher over the radio, I leaned my head against the window. The car ride was never-ending. The path taken to the precinct seemed to pass every bus stop and crowd where people could potentially see me and judge me for what I'd done, except I was innocent this time. Blood coated the window from my forehead injury, and the gash seemed to bleed out more as the tires hit several potholes in the street. The handcuffs dug into my wrists, no doubt causing my skin to chaff and rip open.

I winced and moaned in agony. The cops only laughed, refusing to look back or acknowledge my pain. If I turned just slightly to the left, I could see Cordell's vehicle several cars behind with Randi in the passenger seat. They had been ordered to come down for additional questioning.

This was embarrassment at its finest.

As the squad car finally reached the precinct, I held my breath in anticipation. God was much bigger than any of my problems, no matter how bad they looked. I said my prayers and waited to be removed from the vehicle. But I could not lie—my nerves were everywhere and any positivity I had initially was now slowly diminishing.

Another car, other than Cordell's, zoomed up beside the squad car. One of the arresting police officers stepped out with his hand on his gun defensively. Unsure of whom it could be, I squinted to avoid the thick stream of blood from entering my vision.

The other cop turned to me smugly, ordering, "Stay right here. Oh, wait, you have no choice but to stay put, *sicko*."

I grimaced at his cruel words and kept my eyes on the outside world, tuning into the voices beyond the window. Another employee whom I had not met before but saw around the office came rushing towards the squad car. She was running as quickly as her short strides and high heels would allow.

"Wait! Wait!"

"Ma'am, can we help you? This is a restricted area. The front of the precinct is where you should be."

"Marie, why did you leave the office? This is a private matter that doesn't concern you," Cordell interjected.

"Private matter? Everyone saw this man be detained from the building. There was nothing private about his arrest. What are you detaining him for? Were his rights read to him before you took him away? My husband's an attorney, so I know HIS rights!" The woman was passionate as she spoke, and her eyes were narrowed in fury.

The officers looked around in confusion, as did Cordell. "I'm afraid we can't divulge that information, ma'am."

Randi looked on in disgust, eyeing the woman. "Why are you protecting a pedophile? He was looking at child pornography—that's why he's been arrested."

"No, no, I can't let you take away this innocent man. I sit across from his office and I saw his ENTIRE day unfold. He did not watch any pornography, or even turn on his monitor, other than trying to sign up for our company emails and access his headset. While she 'trained' him," the woman said sarcastically, pointing at Randi, "he was a complete gentleman. On the other hand, Randi was very suggestive and brushed her hands and body parts against him on a couple of occasions. She's lying! It's the same reason the other guy probably quit after two months. She accused *him* of assaulting her, remember? There was no real proof then and there's no proof now. Your daughter's driving these men out because she can't stand rejection!"

Everyone grew quiet, as her words seemed to echo throughout the afternoon air. The police officers looked around, mostly at Randi and Cordell, and then back at me in the car, suffering in silence. Cordell rushed to speak, grabbing ahold of his daughter's arm.

"Randi, is this true? Did you lie on Jalen?"

"Check his computer monitor!" she ordered through gritted teeth. Tears rushed to her eyes and she favored a rich, spoiled brat in that moment.

"RANDI! Is…this…true?" Cordell questioned for a second time, while balling his fists up at his side. "Randi Latonya Stacey, answer me right NOW!"

Instead of answering, she closed her eyes, stomped her foot like a child, and then screamed at the top of her lungs. Everyone winced, knowing she had just told on herself. I, on the other hand, could smell a lawsuit. I had been wrongfully accused, terminated, and incriminated without any evidence for the accusations. I watched as everyone's expression changed from stern to apologetic, including Cordell's, but I just wanted to get out of the cuffs and go home.

The once smug officer that drove the car walked back over and opened the door. The handcuffs were taken from my wrists and the officer spoke remorsefully, "We're so sorry, Mr. Owens. Let's get you a bandage for your head and wrists, and someone can take you back to your job."

I said nothing in return and ignored their gestures as I examined the gashes on my wrists. I needed something to soak up the blood, but at that point, I wasn't going to waste another second of my life with the same people who had taken away my dignity and self-respect minutes before.

"I'll take a bus."

"No, *I'll* take you back," Marie, the employee who had saved the day, spoke, "It's no problem at all. Let's get you your belongings. For goodness' sake, why don't you have on shoes? Oh, this precinct will definitely be hearing from my husband! This is preposterous."

About three hours later, and after filling out stacks of non-disclosure agreements regarding the incident, I was free from the workplace and entering into the house. Randi had been charged a hefty fine for her false accusations. Cordell begged me to stay on board as a staff member, promising to fire his daughter and raise my pay rate for the troubles. I accepted, but only on a couple conditions; he would have to promote me to her old position and give me an advance on my paycheck. Otherwise, I planned to sing like a canary to the local news station. Surprisingly, he agreed and told me he would have another staff member train me in the morning.

As I walked towards the bedroom, I noticed Summer was dancing to music, while Autumn was attempting to cook dinner for all of us. She was making our favorite—breakfast food. I could smell turkey bacon, sausage, scrambled eggs, and buttery biscuits. Even with my eventful day, I managed a soft, grateful smile their way.

"How was work, Dad? Did you like your new job?" Autumn questioned, peeking into the oven. "I hope you're hungry."

"I'm starving, baby girl," I admitted, purposely not answering parts of her questions. I decided that I would not let them in on what happened, but I had to come up with an excuse if they noticed my wrists that were still raw and bloody from earlier. I shoved my hands in my pockets self-consciously. "I didn't know you girls could cook so well."

"Autumn can. I can't. I just know how to eat," Summer joked, turning off her TV program.

I chuckled and pulled out my buzzing phone. Now that I was home, it seemed all my missed calls and text messages were coming through. I scrolled through and selected one phone number in particular. It was an apartment manager returning my call about a vacancy in late August. It was around the price range I was going for, in a decent neighborhood, and had the right number of bedrooms and space I needed. My application had also been approved. I retreated to the bedroom and called the woman back to setup an appointment to see one of the available apartments with a similar layout that I liked. I was reminded of Job in the Bible, in that moment. When all seemed to be lost, God had stepped in and restored everything.

"Good news, girls," I said, clapping. "Daddy will have us a new place in no time."

"I love it here, though. I wish we could stay forever," Autumn pouted, while she stirred around in the steaming skillet. Its aroma wafted upward, hitting our nostrils. "But I know Miss Jamaika probably won't allow that."

I crept closer to peer into the iron skillet. In addition to the other food, she had also prepared some sort of egg, sausage, and red pepper mix. I took my chances and grabbed a few pieces of the sautéed concoction, tossing it back into my mouth.

"Well, I won't allow it either. She was nice enough to let us stay for as long as we have, but I wouldn't want to overstay our welcome. Our new place won't be as spectacular, but it'll be special, and something we call our own," I added, chewing speedily so that I would not get burned. "Baby girl, this is by far your BEST dish."

"Think so, Daddy?"

"I know so. You put your foot in it!"

"Well, I'm glad you like it! With that being said, dinner's ready!" she announced, making plates and setting them on the table. "Daddy, you get to have extra, since you've started your new job."

"Appreciate you, baby girl," I spoke, truly grateful for such beautiful little women. A year ago, I would have never imagined how life would change so drastically but having them in my life full-time had literally saved my life. "I appreciate the both of you. I hope you know how much I love y'all."

"We do, Daddy. And we love you too!" Summer smiled. "Now, let's EAT!"

Chapter Eleven

Time had a mind of its own and moved along quickly. My new job became my favorite place, besides home, of course. It had been exactly two weeks since the time that I marched into the doors of *Stacey & Associates* and made a name for myself *literally* with the whole Randi situation and foolish accusations. Cordell, in spite of his daughter's actions, was now a mentor of sorts, and I knew I could call on him for any advice or work-related issues.

Some may have called me crazy to stay at a job that had falsely accused me of such an atrocious crime, but I also knew God hadn't brought me this far for everything to crumble. Unless He said to move, I wasn't going anywhere. After all, I had quickly fallen in line with the company's culture and fallen in love with my work duties and coworkers. As of this morning, training was officially over, and it was time to dive into the real deal. But first, I needed nourishment.

I sat now in what had become my favorite spot to have lunch. It was a few feet down from the bench that I'd been berated and humiliated on, and in fact, if I looked closely, I could see a very light trail of dried blood near the curb from my injuries. It was baffling that it had not been washed away since then. Despite the pain that day, it also was a reminder of how far I'd come in a short time. I was determined to keep pushing forward.

Crossing my legs at the ankle, I gazed around the area and enjoyed the touch of humidity in the air. The warmth was much needed after freezing for the better part of the morning in my office with the blasting air conditioning. I had an hour to enjoy the turkey sandwich, plain chips, and energy drink I'd packed this morning and chewed leisurely, savoring the tastes. Later this afternoon, I was scheduled to finally view the apartments that I had been eyeing for some time. They were in high demand, but I was thrilled that there were still vacancies. After work, I planned to scoop up the girls and ride over.

I had faith and knew our future home was just waiting to be claimed. As I envisioned the layout and where our furniture would go, the sunlight that had been hitting the side of my face was blocked as a figure approached. I cupped a hand over my forehead, looked up, and nearly choked on my wheat bread at who stood before me.

"What are you doing here?" A tinge of panic could be heard in my voice, I'm sure. "I hope it's not to start trouble. This is my new job, and…"

"I know. I know *everything*…and I came here to apologize and set some things straight," Kyla spoke softly, playing nervously with the ends of her bright, orange-colored hair. "May I…sit down?"

I scooted to the opposite end of the bench and motioned for her to have a seat. Then I checked my watch. "You have about 15 minutes to talk before my break is over."

"All I need is ten."

I admired her from her feet up. Everything was larger with her baby weight. Her breasts, lips, hips, and even feet were swollen, and she glowed like any expecting mother would, but there was a darkness to her eyes. She collapsed slightly onto the bench and dug around in her purse that matched her hair while I looked on, shaking my head at her fashion choices and hair color choices.

Kyla was always so gaudy and flashy, and although she had a beautiful face, some colors just weren't acceptable in my opinion. Kyla was notorious at changing up her wigs and hair, and I would not be surprised if this time next week she wore purple-colored hair or green, or blue. There was nothing professional or appealing about it, in my opinion, but thankfully, Kyla did not have a regular nine-to-five like most people. She could get away with her styles because she worked briefly at the barbershop my brother and I once co-owned.

In fact, that very barbershop was where I met her and fell in love with her body as she strutted around in tight leggings and a crop top, bending over to grab supplies, and looking back to see if I noticed. With a husband as psychotic and overprotective as hers, I was surprised she pranced around so loosely, flirting and coming onto men.

I shook my head to free up my thoughts from those ungodly yesteryears and times when I simply didn't have a clue on what was right and wrong. I looked down at her frantic fingers as they sifted through the faux leather handbag. The last time she dug deep within her messy purse, an ultrasound came out. I held my breath and waited for what was to come this time.

"How did you find me?" My question slipped out abruptly, breaking the silence.

She hesitated as she looked up and met my eyes. Then she went back to digging around in her purse that seemed to have an endless bottom. I wondered, what exactly was she searching for?

"I have my sources. I know people who know *you*. This pop-up will be my first and last, but I had to see you and speak with you before I…"

I grabbed her hands gently, pulling them away from the purse. I was sick of watching her dig around. I touched her face, turning it towards me.

"Forget whatever it is you're looking for. Just talk to me. What's going on, Kyla? It has to be important if you tracked me down and found me at a job, I've had less than three weeks. Is it about the…uh, the baby?"

Kyla's face reddened to the point I thought she might burst. She was nodding but her eyes were far off into the distance, beyond my line of vision. Her eyes watered and she fisted her hands in her lap. I sat back a bit, eyeing her up and down, and not trusting the look in her eyes.

"Are you okay? What's wrong?"

"I'm not okay. I'm barely making it. My husband told me what he did to you and I'm so sorry. I can't undo his actions, but I can apologize on his behalf."

"Well, I deserved it after what I did to *you*. I hit you—and for that, I regret and kick myself everyday. He was only doing what any husband would do if his wife was put in that position."

She put a hand to my shoulder, silencing me. "*No*. You didn't deserve it, especially since I've known the truth all along. I purposely went over your house that morning knowing I was trying to set you up, and like the brilliant man you are, you didn't fall for any of it."

"The truth? Set me up? What are you talking about?"

"The baby! I'm talking about this…this entire lie I've kept up. The baby was never yours. I'm not even sure who the father is and won't know until after the baby's here. I knew from the moment of conception I would be in trouble by my husband.

He had a vasectomy years ago, so he obviously didn't impregnate me." Kyla dropped her head in shame. "I was unfaithful and as a result, I have to deal with a baby, whose father I'm unsure of. I was trying to pin the baby off on you because I knew at the very least, you'd step up to the responsibility. But when you threatened an abortion, that's when I lost it. I just…this mess I've made…it's just…"

Kyla could not seem to find the words as she bowed her head, and more tears gave way. Her face was so wet that it looked like she'd been sprayed with a water gun. I opened my arms slightly, unsure of what to do or say. But I was certain she could use a hug, so I embraced her and rubbed her back as she let snot, tears, and whatever else out on the collar of my shirt. I grimaced but pushed aside my pride and selfish reasoning to embrace a woman who simply had nothing more to give.

For several minutes she bawled, and I looked around to see if anybody was looking.

"Shhh, it's okay," I told her.

Finally, Kyla lifted her head and wiped her petite fingers under the creases of her eyes. She looked broken and vulnerable, and as crazy as it sounded, beautiful. I helped her clean her face a bit and watched as she adjusted her maternity clothes in silence. I went back to gazing out at the picturesque landscape while she gathered her thoughts. There was a peace that settled in the atmosphere. I knew that if I felt it, Kyla definitely should have.

"Thank you, Jay. I really needed that." She sighed and shook her head. Her eyes were still watery, but the waterworks had stopped for the moment. "I can't believe I just did that."

"I'm not trippin' about you crying and getting it all out. Sometimes we all just need a good cry and someone to talk to. But what I *do* want you to do is figure this thing out, Ky. Don't get me wrong. I'm not kicking you while you're down or accusing you of doing something you're not. But this little game you're playing? You have to come clean to your husband. You have to be honest with him. If you love him like you say, then that man deserves to know."

"Heh," she chuckled dryly, continuing to wipe at her face periodically. "That's exactly it. I'm sick of him. No—correction: I *hate* him. Jay, I'm married to a man I no longer even love."

Kyla was dropping bombs left and right. I checked the time on my watch and knew the issues she was discussing would take much more time than I could give. Although I needed to get back to work, I also could not leave her hanging. The poor woman was pouring her heart out and seeking guidance.

"Listen, I've got to get back to work but I promise you, we'll be in touch. Let me figure out some things first, okay?"

Kyla nodded, standing to her feet with reluctance. There seemed to be a weight lifted off her shoulders as she draped the straps of her purse over an arm and hugged me a final time.

"Thank you. Thank you for being a stand-up guy."

I worked until my mind was on overload and my voice was slightly raspy from speaking to potential and existing clients. While most of the coworkers planned to meet up later for chicken wings and beer, I declined.

"You've got other plans, eh?" Bradley asked. He was a young, good-looking white guy with the world at his fingertips, it seemed. He was a technician for the company.

"A date with two of the city's most beautiful ladies," I bragged.

Bradley lifted his eyebrows in both shock and intrigue. His hand landed on his chest while he took a few steps back. Packing up my workbag and shutting down my desktop, I simply laughed to confirm his questions.

"My daughters, man. I'm referring to my daughters."

"Oh! I was going to say aren't you going to at least share? You know what they say. 'It ain't no fun…'"

"'…if the homies can't have none,'" I completed his thought with another light chuckle. He was a trip sometimes. "Nah, it's not even like that. Have a goodnight, man." Our hands came together in a brotherly clasp before we parted ways.

Even if I didn't have a prior engagement, I had not planned on going to any bar with anyone. I knew I wanted to live right and be a better example for my girls. I made up in my mind to keep things strictly professional between my colleagues and I, and certainly would never be caught in a bar or surrounded by people drinking. I was the only Bible some people would ever see, and despite my past, I wanted to make a difference in others' lives. I wanted to be a walking, talking, and living witness of the goodness of Jesus. I had to let my light shine as I'd failed so poorly to do as a pastor years ago.

During the ride home to grab the girls, I unbuttoned the top of my shirt and allowed my tie to freely hang around my neck. I drummed my thumbs to the smooth jazz floating from the radio, wondering what we could pick up later for dinner. I was half exhausted and half excited to see the scheduled luxury townhomes, and again, prayed for the best. I expected good things to happen this evening. The search for a new home would stop now.

"Hey, Dad!" The girls greeted as they reached the car, one settling in front and the other scooting in the backseat.

"What's up, girls? You two have a good day?" I checked both ways before backing out of the driveway and heading down the road.

"It was boring as usual. We made slime, watched this new vampire show, and did our nails. That's all. What'd you do at work?"

I chuckled and looked into the rearview mirror at Autumn. "I definitely didn't work as hard as y'all."

We made it to the townhomes with about seven minutes to spare. I checked in at the front desk before an attractive black woman appeared with her hand outstretched. Her yellow nail polish was the first thing I noticed as we shook hands, gently but firmly. She held a clipboard close to her chest and wore a royal blue pantsuit with a pair of black slingback heels. Her hair was pinned to the top of her head, but during the course of the day, it was apparent that several tendrils had fallen out to frame her face. A warm smile was spread across her full lips and her light brown eyes sparkled.

"You must be Jalen."

"I am."

"I'm Alani, the property manager and a proud resident here at Parkway Townhomes."

"Nice to meet you, Alani. These are my daughters, Autumn and Summer."

"Hiiii." The girls waved with identical smiles.

"Hi, girls. It's so nice to have you all here. Why don't we get started? We have a model unit you may check out further down the hall here." She looked over her shoulder and motioned for everyone to follow her.

"After you." I smiled.

The townhomes were a mix of newly built and newly remodeled units. Each home offered an indescribable view of the city lights and downtown buildings. The particular one I applied for was a three-bedroom, two-bathroom unit with space for both a living and dining area, and a decent-sized kitchen. A washer and dryer set was available in the unit as well. The scent of fresh paint and recently installed carpet could be smelled throughout the place. Before my very eyes, I could see the entire layout come together.

"This is...just perfect, Alani. Is the price still the same?"

"Yes, it is. In fact, we have a half off first month's rent special going on. I see you've filled out an application already. Was the Misses going to be filling one out as well...or?" She searched my hands for any signs of rings.

"Oh, there's no Misses. It's just me," I clarified, still looking around at the updated fixtures and countertops.

"*Yet*. Dad doesn't have a wife...yet. But he's ready for one," Summer jumped in, raising her eyebrows suggestively.

I nearly choked, feeling the warmth of embarrassment seep into my cheeks and down my spine. I gave a tightlipped smile and muttered through gritted teeth, "*Summer*! Cut it out!"

"*Whaaat*? I was just trying to help. You've been looking at her all night while she showed us the place."

I coughed even more, feeling mortified the more my daughter talked. She definitely had not gotten that jabber-jaw trait from me. I looked to Autumn for help, but she only shrugged and giggled behind a hand.

"I'm so sorry," I apologized, looking at Alani with watery eyes. "Excuse this one here. She knows no boundaries."

"No, no. It's okay, really." Alani blushed and bit on her bottom lip. Then she tucked a thick piece of hair behind her ear. I noticed her ears were adorned with at least four or five piercings. "You have all my information if you're still interested...in the um, townhome, that is."

"Absolutely. Thanks for everything. Nice meeting you again."

We waved a final goodbye and headed out the complex with hopeful hearts. I definitely planned to get the ball rolling on my end so we could move out of our place and start our new lives over for the last time.

"Don't think I'm not done with you," I told Summer. "What made you say those things back there?"

"I'm sorry, Dad. I know it wasn't my place, but she was checking you out and you were checking her out. It's obvious you both were feeling each other."

"And just what do you know about that?" I asked.

"Helllooo, we ARE young ladies. We like boys. We know what it feels like to have a crush."

"You like boys, huh?" I looked back at her. "Who are these boys? What are their names and ages?"

"*Daaaad*. It doesn't matter anyway since we're not going back to our old school. The point is, Alani seems really nice and sweet."

Autumn chimed in, "Yeah, unlike that Marisha lady."

"You girls don't like Miss Marisha?"

"She was okay, but she didn't look at you like Alani did...or even how Jamaika looks at you."

"And what way is *that*?" I prodded, learning more and more as the night went on. My heart skipped a beat at the mention of my ex-wife.

"You know, their eyes light up. I can't really explain it, but Miss Marisha isn't the one for you, Dad."

My heart fluttered now, filled with tiny butterflies. I was blown away by the conversation and the fact that my girls were so observant. It was true—kids noticed much more than most adults would ever imagine. My girls especially were always looking, thinking, and plotting.

If they didn't care for Marisha then that said a lot. I valued their opinions over anyone else's and would take their considerations to heart and be mindful. After all, my girls were here to stay but women would always come and go.

Chapter Twelve

After another productive workweek and a few days of praying and meditating, I decided to meet back up with Kyla to finish our conversation. Considering the difficult situations she faced, attending Tuesday evening church service was a must. The moment she stepped through the doors, I was glad that I invited her. She cried and received one-on-one prayer from one of the church mothers. Afterward, I picked up food for the girls and dropped them off at home. Kyla and I headed to a restaurant to talk things out.

"That's *your* place?" she questioned while sliding into a booth.

I slid in across from her. "No, a friend is letting me stay there while we're in between moving."

"Oh, I was going to say, goodness! I should've never left you, big baller," she joked.

I studied her for a moment. "About that, Kyla. I know you were just joking but I can't apologize enough for playing with your heart, mind, and body. I was in a completely different space mentally and spiritually, and I did anything that would satisfy my soul at the time. I never meant to screw up your life."

"You didn't screw up my life, Jay. We both had our hand in this decision to fool around, so don't ever think you're to blame. In fact, I had some of the best times with you. And I don't just mean sexually but you made me feel alive, important, and like a woman. We both played our parts and it put us in a situation we shouldn't have been, but it was a lesson learned."

We sat in silence for a moment while the waitress brought out glasses of water, napkins, and silverware.

"Did you need more time to look over the menu?"

"Yes, please. Thank you." I smiled.

The woman returned my smile and walked away.

"I want to thank you. I haven't been to church in years, Jay. That was exactly what I needed. I mean, just to be in the presence of God and to be surrounded by true worshippers with nothing but good intentions? That was priceless. I may have to stop by for another Sunday or Tuesday service. I just loved the atmosphere."

"I said the same thing the first time I visited. There's no other place I'd rather be."

Kyla smiled and stared at me for a while, not saying anything. I looked back at her, wondering where her head was. She laughed to herself before speaking, "You know, it's so amazing how God turns things around. You, of all people, have shown me what God can do in just a little time. Even with all your mess-ups back then, there was a calling over your life that could not be denied. You were such an awesome man of faith, and tonight, I saw it all over you again. God has changed you, Jay, and I never want to see you go back to being that man ever again. Don't let this world convert you, you hear me? You're one of the good ones. We need more of you in this world."

Her words took me by surprise as I sat up straighter. "Thank you. I—I really mean it. Yes, He's done some incredible things and I was a fool to ever leave His will, but I'm back now, and I'm trying to right every single wrong I've ever done while I have breath in my body. If He can do it for me, He can certainly do it for you, Kyla."

"Pray for me. I know where I'm supposed to be, but it's just so hard to live right."

"All God wants is your 'yes,'" I assured her, rubbing her hand. "You just have to trust the process. Surrender all to Him and watch your life be transformed."

"I plan to. I just don't want to be a hypocrite that comes to church and doesn't have it all together."

"And the saints do? None of us are perfect. There are pastors with struggles, well, you know that firsthand. There are bishops and deacons who deal with things on a daily basis. Even the pope has dealt with strongholds, I'm sure, but that shouldn't stop you from entering the house of God. You have to know that your problems may be big, but we serve an even bigger God. What worries us and keeps us up at night, God has already resolved on our behalf. That's faith, Kyla...believing even when you can't see it."

"I hear you, Jay. Trust me. I do."

Things grew quiet as she pulled her hand from mine and then placed it on her stomach and rubbed gently.

"You were saying you're no longer in love with your husband. What's going on?"

"Yeah," she sighed and thumbed nonchalantly through the menu. "Everything has changed. He's no longer attractive to me; we don't talk or do the things we used to do. Our relationship has become a routine—a routine that I'm sick of. Somewhere along the lines, he became aggressive, paranoid, and overprotective. Now, I can understand wanting to look out for me, but it's a little *too* overbearing. It's gotten to the point where I've found trackers on my devices and I've spotted people following me. He's hired all kinds of people to check up on me. I'm just…I'm done. All his accusations have made me insecure and pushed me into the arms of other men. Yes, he was wrong…and yes, I was wrong too, but I just want out."

"And you don't feel like you can have this conversation with him? I think, at the very least, he deserves to know why you want out of the relationship."

"It's not that simple, Jay."

"Wait. Has he ever put his hands on you?"

Kyla gave a forced, tightlipped smile and looked down. She nodded while she fingered the butter knife. "Several times too many. That's why I know he'll FLIP out if I tell him about this baby. I was thinking about filing a restraining order. You always see in the movies how asking for a divorce from a crazy person turns out and I don't want to end up dead somewhere, but I'm dying everyday by staying. My back is against the wall."

All I could do was listen. I felt terrible the more she ran down the details of her broken relationship. There was not a lot I could do to help, plus with two daughters who were already down to one parent, I did not want to put myself in a position where my daughters were threatened, or their safety was compromised in any way. I felt for Kyla.

"I don't know him well, and from the few moments I did meet with him, he seemed pretty scary and dangerous. Be careful in all of this. Don't

124

make him suspicious about what you're up to, but in the meantime, you need to go to the police and create a paper trail and let them know what you're up against. Document everything he's ever done as far as the abuse, stalking, and threats. You're no longer living for or thinking for yourself. You're carrying a baby, Ky, and this could be very serious."

"You're right. You're absolutely right." She shook her head and exhaled deeply. "Lord, what have I gotten myself into?"

As we continued to talk while deciding on our meal choices, I felt a hard tap on the shoulder. I half looked over my shoulder.

"Say, man, can you pass me the salt? Ours ran out over here."

"Sure." I reached over to grab the saltshaker and turned back around fully. "Here you are, my man."

Kyla gasped the same time I did. I could hear her whisper the name of Jesus in panic and fear. To my surprise, the barrel of a gun greeted me as the saltshaker I'd been holding crashed to the floor. Holding the gun to my forehead was the devil himself. Kyla's psychotic husband and an unknown man sat in the booth directly behind us. How in the world Kyla and I had not seen them walk in was beyond me. They both grinned wickedly, and their eyes were darker than any other eyes I'd ever seen before. They almost looked possessed.

At the sound of the saltshaker breaking, several heads turned to see what the commotion was about. All around us, chaos broke out. People gasped as they noticed the drawn gun and realized what was going on. Others screamed out and began to run in different directions. Restaurant staff walked out from the back, pulling out their cell phones and calling for help. I, on the other hand, could only focus on the cold steel that pressed against my forehead as I lifted my hands in surrender.

"Easy, brother. Take it easy," I mumbled, feeling my eyes cross as I stared at the gun.

"I ain't your brother! What are you doing here with my wife? Didn't I tell you that if I ever saw you again on the streets, I'd KILL you? Imagine my surprise, getting an alert on my phone that Kyla was out running around again. I followed you two here and obviously I'm not too happy to see this. I'm not happy at all."

"Leonard, you promised you would stop spying on me!" Kyla cried, easing out of the booth. "I'm not cheating! He's an old friend, and we were just having dinner. Put your gun down!"

Her husband motioned for the other guy to corner me while he stood up and grabbed Kyla by the arm. "Old friend? You SLEPT with this guy, or are we suffering from amnesia now? You have no business going out to dinner with anybody, and especially a man who's been in your panties! Little whore! How dare you disrespect me and our marriage this way?"

"Baby, he's a changed man. *I* asked him to meet *me*, not the other way around. He was only trying to talk to me and help me."

"Help you? With what? What exactly can this man advise you on that I couldn't?" If possible, Leonard was even scarier in that moment than when he was tossing me around his office like a ragdoll.

"I'm…I'm pregnant. He was trying to convince me to tell you."

Leonard's eyes widened in shock as the truth seemed to slap him across the face. Apparently, he had not heard a word while seated behind us a few minutes ago. He yelled out suddenly and saliva flew from his mouth in all directions. He favored a madman as he slammed his gun against the side of her face until she fell backwards. Her screams of agony rang throughout the already raucous restaurant as people continued to flee left and right. I was almost sure I heard her head slamming into the table on the way down. I attempted to turn around to make sure she was okay but was shoved towards the back of the restaurant by Leonard's sidekick.

"See what minding your own business could've done? But naaah, you had to get involved in another man's affairs, and now look at you," the man berated with his warm, funky breath tickling the back of my neck. "They say you're a man of God. Well, where is your God now? How's He gonna save you now, punk?"

I ignored his words and continued to walk aimlessly past unauthorized areas and into the kitchen where there was no more kitchen staff. Everyone had run out by now with all the chaos, leaving behind food that was still cooking, baking, and sizzling. The kitchen was steaming hot and caused immediate sweat beads to pop up along my forehead.

"Where am I walking to?"

"Just keep walking," he ordered, pushing the gun into my lower back.

I kept my hands in the air as we maneuvered around the kitchen. In about 30 seconds, we would be passing by a sous chef station where several large knives and a few chopped onions sat. Leonard's flunky had a gun, and I had a 50 percent chance of successfully grabbing a knife and defending myself.

What started out as a beautiful night of redemption, forgiveness, and healing, had quickly become a fight for life over death. I thought about my options as we neared the table. For the second time in a short while, my life flashed before my eyes. I thought about my girls and our new life that awaited. I thought about Kyla and her unborn baby and felt sad that she was out there fending for herself.

"Aye, man, can you tell me what this is about? Let's just talk for a second. Put your gun done for a second and let's just be reasonable here. You're the one with the weapon; I don't have anything on me. Let's just talk, man."

He seemed unsure as he thought about it, eyeing me up and down.

"Feel free to check me." I turned with my back to the sous chef station and stretched my arms out from side to side and placed my feet apart.

He patted me down as though he were a TSA agent, searching for narcotics. As he got to my feet and bent forward to dig around in my socks, I reached back and grabbed the knife from the table. I turned it quickly in my clammy fingers, gripped the handle with all my might, and brought it down on his back. I could hear and feel the way the knife pierced through flesh and bone.

Blood splattered on my face as I took the knife out and came down again on his back. He let out a low groan, dropped the gun he held, and stayed facedown on the floor. I could see a slight twitch in his body as blood poured from his three-inch wounds. Whether I'd killed him or not, I did not know, but the knife had served its purpose.

I kicked the gun from out of his reach in case he had the strength to grab it, and then tucked it in my suit jacket. Cautiously, I headed out of the kitchen to see where Kyla and Leonard were. I prayed silently that she was still doing okay. Their arguing voices greeted me as I peeked from the swinging kitchen door.

Leonard was crouched with his back to me. He sat a few inches above Kyla where she lied on her side, gripping her stomach, and coughing up blood. I could not see any gunshots wounds, nor had I heard any gunshots ring out. Her head was bleeding profusely, and she was losing a lot of blood by the second. He must have hit her over the head a few times. Police sirens could be heard outside, so I knew one of the restaurant-goers had gotten ahold of 911. Now I just needed to make sure Kyla was okay and as far away from Leonard as possible.

I snuck up behind him on tiptoes while he ranted, yelled, cursed, and spat everywhere, "You didn't think I noticed you were getting FAT? You think I'm stupid? I knew all along you were pregnant. I was just waiting on *you* to confess! Who was it, Kyla? We've established it isn't that fake pastor's baby…so whose is it?"

Kyla's hair was stringy and matted, clinging to her sweaty, bloody face. She coughed a moment more and was finally able to compose herself and spoke weakly, "I'm not 100 percent sure, but I think it's Larry's."

"Larry?" Leonard stood upright and began to pace. "Larry—my brother?"

Kyla nodded, running the back of her hand across her forehead. "Leonard, *please* get me to a hospital. Let's talk later. I'm…I'm dying."

"You screwed my brother? You dirty...stinking...little...WHORE! Ahhhh!"

As I closed in on Leonard, it was obvious he was in the process of blacking out. He stopped pacing like a madman and then pointed the gun at Kyla, and without any remorse or hesitation, he fired away. Bullet after bullet left his gun and entered her body, riddling her clothes and flesh with holes. She barely could get a scream out before her life, and her unborn baby's life, slipped away before my very eyes.

"KYLA, NOOOO!" I shouted. Composing myself enough to push aside the images of her horrendous death, I went in for the kill. It was now or never. I wasn't able to save Kyla, but I could at least save myself by wrestling with Leonard for his weapon. As I jumped on his back and restrained his arms, we fell to the floor and rolled around. He still held onto the gun with one hand while I shielded my face from the blows of his other hand.

Leonard straddled me suddenly, stopping me in my tracks. Clumsily, I dropped the gun that I'd wrapped my hand around. It slammed into the floor and slid about two feet away—two feet too far from my reach. I was screwed; my only chance at semi-protecting myself was gone. He had the upper hand.

Defeated, I put my hands in the air and stared back at his cold, lifeless eyes. If he could murder Kyla with an unborn child, without thought, I knew my chances of having an open casket funeral were slim to none. I only prayed that my daughters would stick with God and each other and become successful women someday.

I closed my eyes, feeling his stare and the coolness of the gun now pressed to my head. He spoke lowly in my ear, taunting me with the evil things he wanted to do, but I heard none of it. I focused on preparing myself to see Jesus. I prayed a final prayer for salvation and silently hoped I'd righted all my wrongs. That thought comforted me, if only for a moment, as I waited for the click that could end it all.

"Church boy, I've had enough of you..." he snapped, positioning his finger. "All your little sins have finally come back to haunt you. I'm getting turned on just thinking about being the one to give you your just reward."

As he spoke his last words, he shoved the gun into my partially opened mouth and pulled the trigger. *Click.* I continued to breathe shakily and sweat profusely. I opened my eyes, blinking and looking around. Leonard pulled the trigger again...then a third time. And a fourth.

Yet, I was still alive, and nothing had taken my life prematurely.

"Die, already!" **Leonard** shouted, and as he finally lowered the gun and took a few shots in frustration, two bullets were released and entered the floor, damaging it. Remnants of concrete flew up, nearly hitting our faces at the close impact. It was like the gun had been jammed for a divine purpose.

While he remained distracted and confused at the fact that I was still standing and untouched, I lunged for him again and tackled him. I bent my arm and pressed it firmly against his neck, choking him. We struggled on the floor as I pressed my available fingertips into his eyes, blinding him for a moment.

"Ah!" he cried, trying to kick out.

"You're lucky I don't want Kyla's death to

be in vain. Otherwise, I'd choked you out now. I'm going to wait for the police to arrive so they can put you away and you can think about the lives you just took. She was expecting, man! How could you murder your own wife?" I spoke with tears in my eyes, looking back at Kyla's slain body.

With little breathing room and mobility, Leonard had no other choice but to lay paralyzed as I continued to hold him and partially sit on top of his chest and arms. The police arrived within minutes and only until there were handcuffs around Leonard's wrists did I feel comfortable enough to let him go and take him from my sight.

I stayed in the restaurant, in a booth, furthest from Kyla's body that had now been covered with a dark black sheet. Amid blood and broken glass, I answered as many questions as I could about the night. I was transparent and told the detectives everything I knew; I even tattled on myself and detailed the brief relationship that Kyla and I shared, and the possible connection as to why Leonard snapped. I also directed them to the kitchen where Leonard's assailant was crouched in a pool of blood. I assumed I'd murdered him, but he was actually still struggling to breathe with the knife still lodged in his flesh. *Good.* He, too, could be rightfully charged for his actions.

"Thank you for all your help, Mr. Owens. Here's my business card. Please be in touch in case any additional information is needed."

"Thanks," I said, giving a weak smile.

"Sir! Sir!" A woman approached me with a disheveled appearance and a microphone in hand. "I live a few blocks away and ran to work when I heard what was going on. I'm sorry. Let me back up

132

and introduce myself. I'm Sandra Anderson from your local WHAS Channel 26 station."

I accepted her handshake. "Hi, Sandra. How can I help you?"

"I know it's been an eventful evening, but would you mind if we filmed you for a moment as you detail the night's events? It will only be for a few minutes as part of our breaking news segment."

At that point, I was drained. I was ready to go home and hug my girls. I was ready to strip away all my clothes, shower away my anxieties and sweat, and lie under the air conditioning until my heartbeat returned to normal and my body temperature cooled. But the woman's face was so sincere and filled with concern that I agreed.

"Sure. What do you need me to do?"

She had me carefully recite my name, along with its spelling, to one of the news station producers. Then she angled me to stand with the once bustling but now ravaged restaurant in the back of me. The cameraman positioned his camera on me and began a silent countdown with his fingers. *Three…two…one*. Soon, a flash shone upon my face. We were live and on-air for everyone to see. I gulped, feeling a knot in the pit of my stomach.

Maybe I shouldn't have agreed to this, I thought.

The woman took a deep breath and began to speak, "Good evening, and thank you for tuning in to our breaking news report. Tragedy has struck the city in an alarming way. Allegedly, residents in the downtown area heard commotion and shots fired more than 30 minutes ago inside of Sasha's Steakhouse."

As the woman continued, her 'news' voice was rich and clear, with a solemn undertone, "As you can see behind me, the beloved family-owned restaurant now sits in shambles. When police arrived, they found a tragic situation, but thanks to the help of one man, that tragedy has turned to triumph. I'm standing here now with Jalen Owens, who was a first eyewitness. Sir, can you describe what happened here tonight?"

I looked at Sandra, taking a deep breath. "A madman...excuse me, I mean *an upset husband* held up a restaurant and killed his wife this evening."

"Did you know the gunman?"

"Not personally. I was having dinner with his wife, who was an old friend of mine. He pulled out the gun and eventually killed her. Then I tackled him and got the gun from him. I waited until police arrived before letting him go," I explained, looking into the camera nervously, unsure if I had said too much.

"You're being called a hero tonight by witnesses."

I shook my head forcefully, correcting her, "I'm no hero. I'm just a man who wanted to make it home to see his daughters."

"Thank you for your quick thinking and heroic actions. You may not see it that way, but who knows how many lives you may have saved by subduing the gunman?" Sandra gave a reassuring smile.

I was quiet as I nodded and shrugged.

"Well, we see that you are still shaken up. Any last words?"

"As a former pastor, I have to offer these spiritual words of advice." I looked directly into the camera, speaking, "The devil is working hard to destroy us, but God is working even harder to save us. Life can be here one moment and gone the next.

Consider salvation and live your best life…in God and in His will. As for the city, we need to be praying more than ever in these days and times. Summer and Autumn, Daddy will be home soon."

"Very well, sir. I'm so sorry this happened here tonight. Thank you for speaking with us, and for sharing those encouraging words." The news reporter turned towards the camera fully and I stepped out of the frame.

"There, you have it—the firsthand account of one of the two victims of tonight's shooting. Another victim, who was pronounced dead just after 11 o'clock tonight, is described by police as an African American woman in her late 30s. Until family is notified, we will keep her identity under wraps. This is Sandra Anderson from WHAS Channel 26 with your breaking news report. Stay tuned for more updates."

Once the red light turned off, I was given the cue to leave. I walked off from the media crew and limped to my car. There, I sat for several minutes, crying and letting out every emotion, from sadness to anger to confusion. I could not help but to punch the steering wheel with all of my might, injuring my knuckles and hands even more. I was sure that tomorrow there would be all sorts of aches and pains, and bruises. There was also one other thing that I knew for sure. God was yet in control and I couldn't question Him. He had allowed me to walk away with my life.

For that, all I could utter was "*thank you*" as I made my way home.

Chapter Thirteen

When I arrived home, my girls were waiting for me near the driveway. They looked frantic and alarmed as they ran towards my slowly approaching vehicle. I could see tears already streaming down their faces. I turned off my headlights and leapt out of the car.

"Daddy! We saw the news!" they cried in unison. Their eyes were one of my favorite features on them and to think I was at risk of not seeing them ever again brought tears to my own eyes.

We all embraced and cried openly; I held them until I could no longer lift them in my tired arms. Gently, I placed my girls back on their feet and wiped each of their faces and told them how much I loved them.

"Daddy will NEVER leave you. Girls, do you hear me? As long as I have breath in my body, I will NEVER leave."

As we all separated, someone cleared her throat with a sniffle. I looked over and was surprised to find Marisha there with a concerned look on her face. She had wrapped her arms around herself and was rocking back and forth. She wore all black clothing and boots, favoring a tomboy in that moment, but beauty still radiated her soft features. Her hair that was normally bold and luscious, had been combed back neatly into a simple ponytail.

"Marisha? What are you doing here?" I continued to hold onto my girls while I looked at my lady friend in confusion.

"I came to make sure you were okay. I saw the breaking news report and rushed right over. Is everything okay? How are you feeling?" Her face was a mixture of relief, concern, and another emotion that I could not read. "Oh, my goodness. All this blood. Let's get you inside and washed up. Where are you bleeding? Do you need an ambulance?"

"Mari…*Marisha*!" I said sternly, stopping her in her tracks. She had nearly dragged me into the house by my arm. I gently pulled my arm from her hands, assuring her, "It's not my blood."

"Oh." She looked me over and then jumped into my arms suddenly. I felt like a child being looked over and examined by his mother, the way she touched my face and made sure everything was still intact. "You don't know how much I was worried about you. It's so good to hear…and see…and feel you again."

I gave a genuine smile and held her in my arms, allowing her to fuss over me a bit. Her antics halted only when Summer tapped me on the shoulder. "Uh, Dad? Can we go in the house now? These mosquitoes are eating us up out here!"

"Yeah, let's go, girls." I chuckled and motioned for them to walk ahead of me while I locked up the house and made sure everything was safe and secure. Although **Leonard** was now in police custody and probably would not see the light of day for decades, I still felt a sense of paranoia, as though we were being watched.

Finally closing the last blind, I turned back around to where Marisha still stood. "Go ahead and get showered and relaxed. I'll make you all something warm to drink and we can watch a movie or something," she suggested.

I did as told, happy to have an extra set of eyes and hands in the house. The girls agreed to help Marisha around in the kitchen, helping her locate where the mugs were. Their soft chatter followed me into the master bedroom where I showered away the stresses of the day, and changed into a comfortable pair of sweatpants and socks.

I was still in shock but after dousing my face with cold water, reality finally set in. I looked in the mirror for what felt like forever, shaking my head and willing away the images of tonight's shooting. Hours ago, Kyla was alive and well, and talking my ear off. Now, her corpse was in someone's morgue, growing colder and stiffer by the minute.

"*I'm sorry, Ky,*" I whispered sadly. "I'm so sorry."

I left my shirt off, still feeling warm with the adrenaline pumping through my veins. Marisha and the girls made a hot chocolate and a pan of cinnamon rolls. I settled down in the living room loveseat with a small plate in my hand and Marisha joined me, nestled against my side. She handed me a mug that she had already garnished with large marshmallows. I thanked her, taking a generous gulp.

She bit into her sweet roll. "I hope you're okay, and not just saying it."

"I'm alright. This all means a lot to me that you came over here and checked on us. It feels good to be thought of."

"Of course. It's been a while, but you've never left my mind. And nights like tonight force me to realize a few things," she said, dabbing glaze from her mouth with a napkin.

"What's that?"

"I realize how much I care for you, and…and how much I really need you in my life. I can't stop thinking about you or what we could be." She ducked her head, avoiding my eyes as she continued, "When this happened tonight, I couldn't help but feeling like a fool for not taking that next step with you. It would've killed me never to see you again…or get the chance to kiss, hug, and love you."

I was taken aback by her words but chose not to let it show. We had previously discussed building a friendship and keeping things platonic until life said otherwise, so I was surprised to hear her confession. Marisha looked nervous as she professed her feelings, probably hoping I didn't reject her. Despite my daughters saying they did not think Marisha was the one for me—in that moment—I was smitten. I could admit that it felt good to have a woman tell me sweet nothings; after all, it had been a while since I last heard them. I studied the side of her face, not saying anything and allowing my silence to speak for me.

"Do you…feel the same?" she blurted. "Talk to me, Jalen."

I placed my plate on the table, clearing my throat. As I wiped my hands and figured out my next words, Marisha sat back further on the couch. I thought about the night's events and how tired I felt. No matter how good her words sounded, Marisha was forcing me to have an in-depth conversation in this moment and it wasn't necessarily fair. All I wanted was my bed and to ease my mind from the tragedy and madness that had taken place, yet here we were. I stared back at her with as much intensity as she gave me, sighing.

"Given the day's events, I just…I just want to chill with you and have a peaceful night. Can we have that? Can we save the deep discussion for another day?"

"Woooow," she stretched out the word and looked offended as she rubbed her hands up and down her thighs. "I guess I have my answer."

"Don't do that. Please don't do that, Marisha. You know from our previous conversations how I feel about you. But I just want...no, I *need* peace right now," I rushed to explain, pulling one of her hands from her thigh. "Look at me, sweetheart."

Marisha reluctantly looked up, favoring a reprimanded child. I pushed a few stray hairs from her face, brushing them with my fingertips backward into her ponytail. I smiled at her, admiring how lovely she looked. Even in her casual state and all black clothing, she was stunning and certainly would have turned heads if we were out and about in the city. I especially loved the plumpness of her lips as she called herself pouting.

"Stop that," I encouraged, rubbing a thumb over her lips until she relaxed them completely. "I *do* care for you...and you're something special to me. I need you in my life just as much as you need me. But let's not complicate things or put a title on things. Let's just enjoy each day, getting to know each other better, and figuring things out as we go along like we originally said. I'm not playing games, and I know you aren't...we're both adults here...let's just do what we do. Agreed?"

Marisha seemed to think about it and nodded, offering me a small smile that reached her eyes.

"Agreed. I'm sorry...I just..."

"Shhh," I silenced her first with an index finger to her lips and then kissed her softly. For a moment, our lips touched sensually in a slow dance.

I cupped her face gently and angled her head, holding her in place as I spoke with my mouth.

As we continued to kiss, her hand came up and rested against my bare chest. She moaned slightly, coping a quick feel of my hardened muscles and then nonchalantly trailing downward to my abdomen. I took that as a cue to break apart. Emotions were already so high and all over the place. We didn't need to fall into this kind of temptation, and especially not when I was on a straight and narrow path.

Sex and forced intimacy was usually how it would go with me and a beautiful woman, at least back in the day. Although I was a changed man, I still wanted to steer clear of anything that would put me back to my heathen days. I promised God and myself that the next woman I made love to would be my wife, and not a second sooner. Whether Marisha and I made it to that point or not, I still was not willing to take the risk. Her lips tasted amazing, but that was all I wanted to taste for the time being.

"It's late, and I need to get you home to your girls," I told her, looking towards the clock mounted on the wall. I rubbed the hair along my chin, looking back at her. "Would you like me to trail you home?"

Marisha breathed heavily, her chest moving up and down rhythmically. "No. I…I can call for a ride, or something."

"Oh, you didn't drive?"

"My partner dropped me off," she said before looking like she had been caught doing something she should not have been doing. "I mean…"

"Partner?" An eyebrow lifted.

141

"I meant best friend. You know, my partner in crime," she rushed to correct me with a nervous smile.

"Then it's settled. I'll take you home. I'd be less of a gentleman if I allowed you to walk out that door and get in a stranger's car."

"No, really, I'm okay. I'm a big girl and can make it home safely." She patted her side, where the imprint of a gun was. My eyes widened while she laughed. "Relax, relax. It's on safety. Plus, I'm certified with classes and a Concealed Carry license."

"Who are you?" I questioned playfully. "You continue to amaze and surprise me the more I know you."

"Hey. A girl's got to do what a girl's got to do...especially with children and no man at home."

"I ain't mad at ya." I headed over to the counter, looking for my set of car keys. The place I remembered putting them somehow came up blank. "What's your plans for tomorrow?"

"Um, just a little grocery shopping and running a few errands."

"No work?" I questioned, picking up stray pieces of mail. "Where are my keys?" I muttered, scratching the back of my neck.

"I thought I saw you put them on the end table earlier. You check there?" Marisha suggested.

"I've checked everywhere. I'm losing it." I shook my head and looked around the room in confusion. After a few more minutes of searching the couches, drawers, and pockets of my pants, we came up with nothing more than dust, a few loose coins, and a bobby pin. "Well, so much for me being a gentleman."

"It's okay, really, Jay," Marisha insisted, leaning in for a hug and one final kiss. "As I said, I am perfectly capable of making it home on my own."

"I never said you weren't," I mumbled against her velvety lips. "I still don't want you out there by yourself, so if you want, you can sleep in my room for the night, and I'll take the couch. I'll arrange a ride for you in the morning."

"Jay, no. I can't let you do that. Your girls are here, and I don't want to send them the wrong message. Seriously, get in bed and relax. Come on. I'll tuck you in," she cooed, tugging on my arm so that I could follow her to my bedroom. "You look tired, and you've had a long day."

"I realize that, but…" I pulled away from her and ignored whatever words came out of her mouth. "…I'm going to grab some of these extra blankets and pillows and make me a pallet in the living room."

"You are not giving up, huh?" She chuckled and looked around in the living room. "Okay, so I'll stay, but the least I could do is be the one to sleep on the couch. You get in your nice comfy bed, okay? I'll be fine out here. I'll just need to know where your office is. Can I at least check my emails before I go to sleep?"

"Always working, huh? That's fine." I motioned for her to follow me. "Now, all the passwords are written on the notepad beside the computer. It's not *my* personal computer, so don't save anything crazy on it. I'll be checking your web history when you're done," I joked.

"Yes, Father," she shot back with just as much playfulness. "Thank you, though, Jay. I appreciate you."

143

"It's the least I could do." I leaned into the doorframe as she logged onto the computer. "You're good?"

"Yes, I'm fine. Have a good night, handsome," she called out, swiveling her slim hips around in the chair.

"You too, beautiful. Have a good night." I winked and headed back to my bedroom. There, I literally stripped down to my boxers and landed flat on my face in a heap of much needed sleep.

Sleep stayed with me well into the morning, past almost one in the afternoon, where it took a hand lightly slapping my face for me to break free from slumber and the nightmares that plagued me. Foamy drool coated the corners of my mouth, and there was stickiness in my eyes. I felt like a ton of bricks had fallen on me through the course of the night. Every muscle in my body seemed to scream out as I rolled to face the owner of the hand who had slapped me.

I expected to see Summer or Autumn playing some overboard joke, but it was not my girls. I even half expected to see Marisha, since she had stayed the night. But it was not my love interest either. It was my ex-wife's husband, Levi, peering over me and looking concerned. "Bro, you were out cold. *Wake up!*" he hissed.

I jumped in surprise and covered my chest with the sheet. "What's…what's going on?"

"Were you given something?" he questioned me like an inquisitive father would his irresponsible son. "Wake up. Do you know what time it is?"

"Hmmm?" I squinted and shielded my eyes from the light that peeked through the blinds. Then, out of nowhere, the blinds opened completely, and caused my eyes to close. I moaned at the discomfort. My head spun like a ballerina and I could imagine that I looked puzzled, disoriented, and inebriated. "Ah! Close the curtains! Close the curtains!"

"Oh! I'm sorry!" the sound of my ex-wife's voice was gentle and apologetic. "I've never seen anyone sleep that hard before. We thought you were dead!"

I continued to hold a hand to my forehead and the other hand nestled against my lower stomach. At any moment, I felt like I could throw up last night's dinner. "What's going on? I know this is your house, but why are you guys here?"

Levi spoke up, looking around at the mess on the floors and countertops. "I'm glad we did stop by. This place is a mess, man. I thought you were going to be keeping up with the house?"

"I have been…I…" Reluctantly, I lifted my head and looked around at what he was referring to. The once clean, well-kept room was now in shambles, as if someone had gone through everything, top to bottom. My clothes were strewn everywhere, and there were papers all over the floor. "What in the *world*? Who did this?"

"Who was the chick you let sleep over our house?" Jamaika spoke up sternly, propping a hand on her hip in annoyance. "That's the BIG question."

"Look, I didn't mean to disrespect your home. She was a lady friend and…"

"A lady friend you knew and trusted? Or someone you just met?" Levi inquired, attempting to pick up a few of the papers.

"We've known each other for awhile now. I let her stay over so that she wouldn't have to leave out in the middle of the night." I sat completely up in bed, running a hand over my face. "What's wrong? Did something happen to her?"

"No, but something definitely will. This lady friend you care for and trust so much is not who you think she is. I was watching her on our security camera early this morning because she set off an alarm in our pool house. Do you have ANY clue what she did?"

Okay, now I was totally lost as I listened to Jamaika explain.

"I don't know what you're talking about."

"What's her name, Jay?"

"Marisha. But I don't understand…what happened? How do you know her? What…what did she do?"

"I knew she looked familiar but just couldn't put a name to her face. Plus, she's about 100 pounds lighter. Just think, Jay. Remember Marisha…or better yet, Sister Johnson's cousin that would visit and try to push up on you in Sunday School? It got so bad you had to kick her out of the church because she wouldn't take no for an answer. She was the *only* female you ever turned down and didn't cheat on me with because you said she was fat and unattractive. Jay…just think about it!" Jamaika commanded, stomping her foot in frustration.

"Marisha…Marisha…" I scanned my mind and thought about all of the women who had thrown themselves at me over the years. There were so many that I honestly drew a blank. "Wait a minute. Sister Johnson's cousin—the one who always wore flat shoes instead of high heels? The choir members would laugh and joke about her and I'd have to keep them quiet in the stands whenever she sang. *That* Marisha? My memory's still a little fuzzy. I can't…I can't picture her."

"Yes, Jay! That's her! She looks a little different with the weight loss, but that's definitely her. How could you EVER forget that crazy woman? To think you had her in my house is sending chills down my spine. Oh, my goodness!"

"But what's the big deal? People change…feelings change. She's not the same person and I'm definitely not the same man. She's a decent woman. What happened?" I slid to the edge of the bed, yanking on a T-shirt in the process.

"Why don't you check it out for yourself? Babe, pull it up on your phone," Jamaika instructed Levi, while she continued to pace around in a pink two-piece jogging suit and matching pink and white tennis shoes. "This is unbelievable."

Levi scrolled through his phone for a moment before handing me the device. I held it with shaky hands, watching as first Marisha was caught on camera putting my keys in her pocket while I showered, and the girls washed their hands in the kitchen. That would explain why I could not find them last night.

"I knew I wasn't crazy! She took my keys!" I shouted.

"Keep watching. That's not all she did," Levi added dryly.

I could literally feel my insides boil and my anger build dangerously high as I continued to watch the action unfold. I watched us kiss and interact before I led her to the office. There, Marisha pretended to log on. But when I walked away, she searched and rummaged through all of the file cabinets, in search of something. Levi pulled up another angle of the camera where Marisha walked out to the driveway and unlocked my car. She looked through every compartment she could before a neighbor walking his dog came up and asked her what was going on.

Politely, Marisha could be seen smiling and making small talk, before the neighbor bade a goodbye. Finally, Marisha's searches ended in the pool house where she only got so far as to opening the door before an alarm went off, alerting the local security officers in the subdivision. She took off running, dropping my keys and a few other stolen items in the process.

My mouth ran dry as I watched the woman I thought I cared for deceive me in the strangest way. Why was she searching through my belongings? Why was she being dishonest and lying? Was her name even really Marisha? Once again, I was left to pick up the pieces and attempt to put them together. Marisha was a mystery, and I was determined to find out why she was doing all these things. Knowing our history, I thought back to when I kicked her out of the church.

"Maybe this is some sort of revenge? I don't know." I shook my head, unable to put together any logistics. My head pounded like a drum. "Can someone pass me the Tylenol? I feel terrible."

"You know why, right?"

I looked at Jamaika in half confusion and half understanding. "No…no."

She nodded. "We caught that part too. She slipped something in your drink while you and the girls were looking away. I'm sorry to be the one to break it to you, but she's no good for you. I don't know what she has on you, Jay, but she's determined to take you down. If I were you, I'd figure out what she was searching for."

That was exactly what I planned to do as soon as I wiped the crust from my eye.

Jamaika and Levi kept the girls busy, along with their own children, while I showered and got dressed. When I joined them in the kitchen, I could hear Levi on the phone calling the police and reporting some items missing from their pool house and home office. Jamaika was also on the laptop, typing away as she sent her security system company a long email about a breech.

The girls looked worried. "Dad, what's going on? Is someone after us?" Summer wanted to know.

"No, baby girl. Nobody's after us. You both are safe with me…and always will be. Don't you worry." I offered a smile as I leaned into the kitchen counter, trying to remain as calm and collected as possible. If I showed worry upon my face, then the girls would begin to stress as well, and I couldn't have that.

"Does this have anything to do with Marisha?" Summer asked, looking me directly in the eye with seriousness I had never seen before. She favored her mother in this moment as she challenged me to lie to her.

I said nothing, trying to decide my next move.

"I knew it!" Autumn jumped in. "Your silence says it all, Dad! We told you Marisha was bad for you! I hated her then and I definitely hate her now! What exactly did she do?"

"Yeah! Why did you trust her, Dad?"

"How did she even know where we lived? *No one* knows that information!"

I felt even worse as my girls berated me with questions that I had no answer to. With all that went on last night, I failed to wonder that very question. How *did* Marisha find out where we lived? I had never brought anyone except Kyla over to the house, and with all the security gates, it would have been impossible for Marisha to figure out how to get in without codes or a gate transponder.

I rested my still pounding head in my hands dejectedly. "I can't believe this. Lord, I can't take anything else happening. What in the world have I done?"

"Speaking of which," Jamaika began to say softly, coming out of the office, "I'm so sorry about what happened to your friend. We saw the breaking news reports yesterday and saw a piece of your interview. It's made national news."

"National news…*seriously*? Within just a few hours? Ugh. I definitely don't need that added attention. God knows I just want to be a normal man without scandal or drama surrounding my life. I've had enough of that for *two* lifetimes," I spoke sadly, rubbing my fingers along my scalp in frustration.

"Well, you truly are a real-life hero. In these days and times, people are killed or injured by gunmen more than ever, so for you to tackle him and keep him down until police arrived, that's admirable, man," Levi added. "Whoa. God must *really* be transforming my heart for me to say that."

Jamaika nudged her husband. "Cut it out. While we get this situation squared away, you should probably call Cordell and update him on everything that is going on. He gave us a call about an hour ago while we were trying to get you awake."

"My job! Oh, shoot! I forgot about it," I groaned, racing to get my phone but not finding it in any of the places I'd left it. My heart fluttered, knowing I had all kinds of pictures, passwords, and important contact information in it. My mind raced a mile a minute, knowing it was probably stolen right along with everything else. "Wait a minute. Where is my phone? Did she take that too?"

"Here. Use mine," Levi offered. "I have him already saved in my contacts."

"Appreciate it, man." I disappeared into the bedroom and explained all that was going on to Cordell. I pleaded for him to give me the next day off while I figured things out and he generously obliged. He seemed more understanding and concerned than angry, so that made me feel halfway decent. Still, I knew this was a new job and I could only get so much grace. Once I recovered from this loss, I couldn't let him down any further.

"Let me know if you need anything from me. Take it easy, man," he told me just before hanging up.

While I still had access to a phone, I searched the Parkway Townhomes website so that I could give the property manager a call. I wanted to setup a time that I could bring in my security deposit and half of first month's rent. Life couldn't stop because of all the foolishness going on; I still had to provide for my family. The property manager answered on the third ring, sounding breathless, as though she'd run across the office to pick up the phone.

"Good afternoon and thank you for calling Parkway Townhomes. This is Alani speaking. How can I assist you today?"

As weird as it was, my stomach jolted at the sultry voice in my ear. "Hey, good morning, Alani. It's Jalen…Jalen Owens. I checked out your properties not long ago and…"

"I remember you," she cut me off. "You and those gorgeous girls. I remember you guys. Hey, Jalen, is there any way you can come in and we can further discuss your future residency here at Parkway? We ran into a bit of a problem during your background check."

Here we go again, I thought. "What kind of a problem?" I asked.

"Well, it came back with a negative report. We don't necessarily discriminate and reject applications, but we do like to know what's going on with our residents to prevent any future disturbances."

"Oh! The arrest…yes." I shook my head, feeling hopeless as I explained myself, "Well, I didn't think it would even show up on my records because it was a poorly conducted arrest recently. A former coworker falsely accused me of something ludicrous. Police arrested me and not even ten minutes later, I was freed to go home. I'm not even sure why it's still on my records."

Alani was quiet on her end and I could hear papers rustling.

"You still there?" I asked, knowing she was. I could hear her breathing softly in the phone.

"Oh, wow. Yes, I am. Give me one second, Jalen." She put me on hold for about two minutes before her silky voice entered my ears once more. "Okay, I believe you. I really do. I'm sorry for the misunderstanding."

"No worries. I can see how it could raise some flags. So…am I okay to rent with you all?"

Typing could be heard in the near distance. "Yes, absolutely! I'm sending everything through right now. You may come anytime between today and Friday evening, and…just ask for me. I'll be here." There was a smile in her voice as she wrapped up the conversation.

I rejoined the group in the kitchen and sat down at the breakfast nook to eat the lukewarm eggs that had been prepared by Jamaika nearly an hour ago. I was sure that my face exemplified how I felt—depressed, sad, and defeated. What Marisha had stirred up seemed to take me back ten steps. But I knew the God I served would not let me down. Like always, he would get me out of trouble and save me from the tricks of my enemies. My only problem was why was Marisha the enemy? Besides kicking her out of church years ago, what was her agenda for trying to ruin my life?

Even while investigators came over and prepared to take fingerprints, check security cameras, and ask a million and one questions, I could not focus on anything but Marisha's possible motive. I traced my brain as far as my memory would allow, sifting through my countless sinful nights, handful of affairs, and the hundreds of women who came ready and willing each service to throw themselves at me. I was once head of a mega church so it would be impossible to remember every encounter, let alone remember a plumper Marisha from over a decade ago.

I recalled the lips I'd kissed in my lifetime and the bodies I'd touched. The memories slapped me like a scorned woman; each time I thought I had it all figured out, I was reminded of another woman who I'd shamelessly, carelessly, and unapologetically hurt. There was no telling what I'd done to Marisha in my yesteryears. I was wrong for so long that there was no way of pinpointing what happened.

"We've recovered your phone. It was out back, thrown in the grass," one of the leading detectives, Gerard Michelson, told me. "I've checked for prints. It came up clean, so you're free to use it."

"Oh, good! Thank you." I examined my phone, front to back, not seeing anything too suspicious or off about it.

"What did we say the perp's name was?" he questioned as his crew uninstalled all of the security cameras with gloved hands and special equipment. He was a heavyset, middle-aged man with a sprinkle of gray hair. For the last few minutes, he'd been quietly scribbling notes on a yellow legal pad and pacing the living room floor.

"Marisha. Marisha Blackman," I clarified, looking him up and down. He favored Forrest Whitaker a bit in stature and the way he talked.

"Why does that name ring a bell?" He looked off into space for a moment, tapping his pen against the side of his face. "Blackman...Blackman..."

"Marisha, the fat woman?" another detective chimed in.

154

I shrugged. "Uh…well, she's not fat currently. Perhaps she was previously, but the Marisha I'm referring to is thin. Stunning woman with…"

"Marisha Blackman…THEE Marisha Blackman that was fired from the department years ago for illegally conducting investigations and securing evidence from crime scenes? It can't be."

"Boss, I wouldn't put it past her," a third detective added.

"Wait, *what?*" I asked, looking around at everyone's puzzled expressions. "Who exactly is she?"

He looked over wearily, sighing, "Son, I'm afraid I can't divulge that information."

"You've already shared more than enough. Come on. I've invited this woman in my home; she's met my kids, and I was developing feelings for her. I feel like this is the least bit of information I could get," I pleaded, looking at Gerard with desperation.

He sighed, motioning for me to follow him outside. He leisurely pulled off his latex gloves and tossed them in a nearby trashcan. He looked off into the distance, speaking lowly, while he eased his thick hands into his front pockets. "Ms. Blackman had issues, plain and simple. She was proficient at her job, but too often, she allowed her personal life to dictate what went on in the workplace. For example, her first suspension came from stalking a former boyfriend of hers. Her second suspension happened when she grew too attached to one of the criminals we detained. The straw that broke the camel's back was about 11 years ago when she took it upon herself to accuse a former pastor of embezzling church funds. Needless to say, her actions drew too much negative attention to the force, and we had to let her go."

An invisible fist seemed to punch me in the gut. I felt sick all of a sudden and knew I would not be able to keep down the breakfast I'd consumed a little while ago. Marisha was exactly who everyone said she was. I remembered it more than ever now. While Jamaika and I were ending our divorce, I had been hit with insurmountable charges. A few of those charges included embezzlement, and from that day forward, I'd been convicted to pay back every cent to the church I once loved and adored. I couldn't believe this was the same woman who had captured my heart. Marisha had committed the ultimate betrayal.

"Yesterday she mentioned something about having a partner…and then tried to correct herself when I called her out on it. She also had a gun on her hip. Is this all from her previous employment or do you think she's working for someone else?"

Gerard shrugged. "There's no way she should she be on anyone else's legal department, but who knows? She's been a bitter, vengeful woman for years. There's no telling what's next from her."

I grabbed onto the detective's shoulder, gripping my chest. It felt like my heart was about to explode.

Gerard held me up in his arms, looking around for help. "Is everything okay, Mr. Owens? Are you having difficulty breathing? Someone call a medic! He might be having a heart attack!"

"No…no, wait. I…I'm okay," I whispered, focusing on getting my breathing under control. I continued to hold my chest and heave. Gerard walked me over to the patio furniture, sitting me down. "As God as my witness, Detective, I want you to find that woman! I want to know why she did this to me…to us. This isn't even my home, and she came in and messed things up. I need to speak to her and find out why."

Gerard rubbed my shoulder and looked me square in the eye, promising, "Mr. Owens, I can assure you. We will do all that we can to find her and to bring you peace of mind."

Chapter Fourteen

With all that was going on, I thought it was best to let the detectives handle their job, while I carried on with my head high. Life could not stop just because of my past mistakes, or someone's ongoing plot to get even. I had a family to provide for and a life to reclaim. Marisha would get her rightful punishment sooner than later. In the meantime, all I could do was trust God and trust the people he'd placed on the investigation to figure everything out.

To my surprise, Jamaika and Levi stayed a few extra days to make sure all security cameras were up-to-date, and all locks had been changed throughout the house. They even went grocery shopping and took the girls school shopping, along with their own clan. I wondered why they were being so generous. I know I had been forgiven, but after everything I'd done in my past that hurt and killed Jamaika's spirit, it was a wonder that they were still so giving, warm, and kindhearted.

While they were away, I decided to stop by Parkway Townhomes to drop off my necessary payments and forms. I was relieved to see Alani. She was dressed in denim shorts and an off the shoulder top that bared her midriff with the right motion. Her hair was combed back into a low bun and sandals were strapped to her pretty, manicured feet. I noticed she was much more casual than the first time we met and wondered if it was Casual Friday at the office or something. Either way, I could appreciate her ability to look just as stunning in denim as she did in a pantsuit.

"Please excuse me," she said, seeming to catch my perusal. "I knew I didn't have any showings today, so I went casual. Plus, my allergies are really bothering me, and I just wasn't feeling the dress and heels I'd prepared."

"You don't have to explain anything to me," I assured her, shaking her hand and allowing her petite fingers to linger in mine. "I hope you feel better. How has your day been otherwise?"

"*Really* slow. Nothing too exciting. How's your day going?"

"It's gotten much better." I bit on my bottom lip slightly as she blushed at my words. "I can't thank you enough for overriding that background check foolishness."

"I'm just glad you decided to stay at Parkway. I think you'll be a great resident here and a perfect fit. We like tenants who are responsible and respectful, and I've seen nothing but that from you."

"I feel at home here," I told her, genuinely meaning what I said. "It was a no-brainer that this would be our next home."

I presented the envelope to her with a cashier's check inside and watched her disappear in the copy room, make a copy of the check, and then file it in one of the cabinets under my *New Tenant* file. She rounded the desk, printed out a quick receipt, and then handed it to me with another million-dollar smile. She could have been a *Miss America* candidate—that's how naturally gorgeous she was.

"You're all set, Mr. Owens."

"Jalen," I corrected. "Please call me Jalen."

"Oh, right. Thank you so much again, Jalen. I look forward to seeing you around here soon."

I began to back out of the room, but something caused me to stop. Knowing I should not have even pulled such a move, I took a deep breath and took a chance, unable to resist.

"If you don't mind me asking, what are you, um…doing later?"

She smiled and smoothed her hand over her hair. Before she could answer, her office phone rang. She looked disappointed as she turned and ran over to answer it.

"Thank you for calling Parkway Townhomes. This is Alani speaking." Her face dropped completely while she greeted the person on the phone unenthusiastically. I chuckled at her expression. "Oh. Hi, Tony."

I allowed her another minute before deciding to head out. She waved a goodbye and watched me leave through the blinds while I tried my best not to look back and offer to take her out to dinner later. I just couldn't help myself. The entire Marisha relationship and stint was still fresh and unsolved, and yet I was already intrigued with another woman. But there was something about Alani that was refreshing and undeniable. Even my girls liked her.

I headed back home with a light heart and saw Jamaika's truck pulling up the road not long after.

"We're *baaaack*," Summer sang, heading up the driveway as I drank coffee and stood in the doorway. "Come help us with these bags, Daddy."

"Did you buy up the whole mall?" I joked, grabbing bag after bag from the girls. This complimentary shopping spree had come right on time. I hated to seem like I needed help, but God knew money was tight and I would need to save up to afford the lawyer I planned on getting to sort out this Marisha situation.

"Just about," Levi mumbled, looking slightly irritated and done with the day. "Never again, I tell you. Never again."

"Oh, hush, baby. It was only five stores."

"Yeah…five stores in SIX hours. We've spent ALL day at that mall. Good luck getting me to *ever* go back there with you."

Jamaika shook her head and poked out her bottom lip. "You mean to tell me you don't like spoiling your wife and kids?"

"I don't mind spoiling y'all, but dang, woman. I need a warning next time! That was torture."

I chuckled at their light-hearted banter and deposited the bags of clothes, shoes, and accessories into the girls' rooms. I went to grab my wallet, coming away with money.

"Just what are you doing?"

I handed Jamaika two twenties. "The least I can do is pay for gas."

"Keep your money. We're good, Jay. It was our pleasure hanging with your little ladies after so many years," she assured me, smiling and rubbing the girls' backs. They looked so comfortable with one another. I remember it was a time when I was married to Jamaika and she would cringe at the thought of being around either of them. After all, they represented my infidelity.

After a few more moments of small talk, and them assuring me that they would contact me if they heard anything else from the security company, Jamaika and her family were off to head back to Michigan.

"Daddy, telephone!" Autumn yelled from the next room over, several hours later, as I washed a few loads of clothes.

I was leaned against the dryer with my elbows pressed to the warm appliance, daydreaming. The sounds of footsteps preceded her as she came running in the laundry room with my cell phone in her hand. It was an unknown number from out of town, but I chose to answer. "Thanks. Hello?"

There was a long pause before I heard anything. "Yeah, uh…Jalen?"

I squinted my eyes so that I could concentrate on the voice. It was sticky sweet and sounded unsure, and instantly boiled my blood. Speckles of saliva flew from my mouth as I yelled her name through gritted teeth. "Marisha!"

Autumn's eyes widened as she heard the name. She crossed her arms defiantly and looked at me with her head thrown to the side.

"What in the world has gotten into you? How could you do me and my family like that?" I asked.

"Listen up, and listen up closely! You have no right to question me! After all you've done to *me*, you have NO right at all to ask me why I did what I did."

I held the phone away from my ear and motioned Autumn to give me privacy. She reluctantly ran off but I didn't doubt that she would go grab Summer so they could eavesdrop in the next room. When she was out of sight, I closed the door of the laundry room with my foot, lowering my voice.

I pretended to be confused. "I'm lost. What did I do to you? All I wanted was to establish a relationship with you…a *friendship*…and build. Why did you go through my things and steal what wasn't yours? I thought we had something special?" Although I was angry, I knew one thing that could calm a deranged black woman down—*compassion*.

Marisha chuckled. When she began to speak again, it sounded like she was outside in the middle of nowhere, walking briskly. "You can save all the theatrics for the next chick you end up with. I was *never* into you. Well, once upon a time, I was, but you wanted nothing to do with me."

"What are you talking about?" I raised my voice slightly, wishing the dryer wasn't so loud. It was hard to hear Marisha and her hushed explanations, so I placed her on speaker. "Marisha, I cared for you."

"Jay, let's just get this all out in the open since you can't seem to understand anything in that THICK head of yours. Let me refresh your memory since you've forgotten everything you *used* to do."

I swallowed hard, keeping quiet. A car door slammed in the background and soon started up. Marisha was now driving, I assumed.

"I came to your church right after you took over as senior pastor. I knew you were married to Jamaika, but I didn't care and had to have you. I admired everything you stood for; you were an example of a strong black man of faith. You were a family man, and a faithful one too…at first. I fell in love with your messages and the way you delivered them, and I wanted nothing more than to gain your attention," Marisha sniffled and laughed bitterly over the phone.

"Eventually, I *did* grab your attention, but it was for all the wrong reasons. The only reason you would talk to me was to apologize for the choir members being rude and laughing at the way I dressed. The only reason you would acknowledge me was to encourage me to keep the faith because I was so depressed from being a FAT, single woman in a church full of skinny and attractive women. No one loved me and no one cared. You didn't even bother to consider my feelings when you kicked me out of the church because of what others thought…not what *I* thought or how *I* felt. You disregarded me and unlike those other women you messed around with, you didn't even look at me twice. Do you know how that made me feel?"

My heart dropped as I heard the anguish and dejection in her voice. The more she talked, the more vividly I saw her as a chunkier woman, standing in the choir stands and looking odd. It was all coming back to my remembrance as I closed my eyes.

"So, what did I do after all that? I lost the weight. I lost the one thing that had held me back for so long. It took me almost committing suicide and getting professional help to realize I needed to dig deeper and see that I was, in fact, worthy and deserving of love, the right attention, and the right man. I didn't need to lose weight to see it, but once I lost the weight, I discovered my self-worth and worked on building my self-esteem. I lost nearly 200 pounds, Jalen, and the world couldn't tell me anything. I looked different and felt different! All the men I had previously chased after began calling me again, and the women who shamed me started to hate on me. I was a new person, and I loved that new person but I still wasn't happy. I still wanted to get even," she continued through her tears. It was obvious that she was crying and reminiscing on her painful yesteryears.

I pressed my back against the door and slid down to the floor. Then I crossed my legs at the ankle, rocking myself side to side. I kept the phone close to my ear so I could hear her loud and clear.

"There were so many people that hurt me. There were so many people I wanted to give a piece of my mind to. I wanted to show off my new body and throw it in the faces of everyone who ever made fun of me! I especially wanted to get back at one man in particular. It was a man who should have handled the situations better. It was a man who was supposed to be professional, understanding, and show compassion…instead, he treated me like the rest."

I swallowed hard, understanding where this conversation was going.

"It was a man who was a pastor and who should've sought God in the matter, but instead, he kicked me out of HIS church! Church isn't supposed to hurt, but *you*…YOU hurt me! You crushed me! You sided with those fools and left me out in the cold. I had no one, Jalen! That church was my life…until you took my membership from me. I felt like I was being punished for being fat and different!"

I openly cried with Marisha now, pressing my hand against my mouth and trying hard to suppress the sobs that racked through my hunched body. My shoulders shook violently as I forced myself to continue listening to her heartbreaking words.

"I looked you up and used my resources from my previous job as an assisting criminal investigator to find you. So, that whole running into each other at the convenience store that day, and all those lies I made up along the way? They were about as real as the wig on my head. I setup all of our chance meetings; wherever you were, I found a way to be there so I could get in good again. That's right. I know you're shocked right now, but there was more to me than blubber! I was intelligent and worked for the local precinct. I had a mind of my own and didn't need you or anyone else to make me feel complete. I found contentment on my own, and I was determined to hurt you like you hurt me. My first investigation on you went south when I presented the department with evidence of your embezzlements, but I later found out, you had already admitted to it and were repaying the stolen funds. But I was determined to find some kind of loophole."

I gripped my cell phone with all my might, seeking to understand her actions. "So why did you carry on the lie? If the first investigation got you fired, why were you trying to get in good with me and play games?"

"Like I said, I was looking for a loophole…something else to drag you down. I wanted to dig up even more dirt on you. For crying out loud, Jalen, you've done everything under the sun. You stepped out numerous times on your wife. You used to beat her head in and humiliated her as a first lady. You slept with just about everyone in our community back then, EXCEPT ME, so surely, you had more secrets. It just sucks that I wasn't able to snoop around and find more. Otherwise, I would've buried you alive, you hear me? I wanted so badly to see you FALL flat on your face. I wanted to get my revenge in a major way, just like you shamed and hurt me in a major way. But that's all over and done with. I've wiped my hands clean with you. I don't forgive you, but I know now that I should've just left well enough alone. You weren't worth my time then or now."

"Marisha....I..."

"I'm not finished. Jalen, I hope you get yourself together and realize all the hurt you've caused so many people. So many women lost their minds because you played with their bodies and their hearts. So many men lost their wives because you came in and damaged their relationships. I hope all that you do from here on out is an example to those beautiful daughters of yours because what you've shown so far is a disgrace," Marisha said with seriousness, no longer sniffling or crying. "*Now,* I'm finished."

"Please don't hang up, Marisha," I spoke cautiously. "Listen, everything you said tonight, I needed to hear. I was wrong, yes…I admit it and own up to it. I realize my poor decisions everyday that I wake, and as much as I wish I could, I can't go back and change anything. I can't change the way I thought back in the day…or change what I did or didn't do. I ruined a lot of lives—my ex-wife and my children's lives were the first ones affected by my infidelity and sin. But God saved me. He healed those strongholds I dealt with and I've been trying to right every move since."

She was quiet on the other end, breathing softly.

"What I *can* say, Marisha, is that I'm sorry for hurting you and making you feel belittled, unloved, and insecure. You were a beautiful woman then and now, and you had no reason to think otherwise. I'm sorry for not standing up for you and defending you against those members who made fun of you. I'm sorry for kicking you out of the church. I'm sorry for failing to have a single conversation with you because I know if I knew the real you then, I would've appreciated you as a woman and as a member of my church. Please say that you forgive me. I was deep in sin and an entirely different man. You *know* I needed help."

She remained quiet for a few more moments. The only sound in my ear was the thump of the dryer and her light breathing. "It will take some time. I do appreciate you apologizing and holding yourself accountable. That was big of you."

"Where are you now?" I prodded. "A different number showed up for you on my phone. I hope you're safe."

"I am safe and very much on the run. I'm not telling you where I am, but just know I'm never coming back. I need to figure things out…in another state," she said with a sigh.

"So, what now, Marisha? You can't run forever. You've done some illegal things, and they'll be after you sooner than later."

"You live your life, and I'll live mine. If that means I have to run until the day I die, then so be it. I've been imprisoned in my mind for so long, so I'm not going to end up in anybody's prison if I have a say so."

I thought about my next words carefully, finally standing to my feet. I felt stiff, sore, and drained. "Marisha, please take care. As I said before, I'm so sorry for the damage I caused in your life. Do what you have to do, but please be safe."

"You too, Jay," Marisha said simply before hanging up on me.

I stared at the phone for another 15 minutes, well after Marisha hung up from me. I felt like I had endured an open-heart surgery. My heart felt raw and torn apart. I also felt physically and mentally drained and exhausted because my emotions were tossed about, and my past had once again come back for a volatile visit. Just when I thought I'd confronted all my demons, I was presented with a few more. I was sure the girls were confused and concerned, and likely listening outside of the door, but I had somebody else to speak to before the night was over.

"Lord, I'm coming to You completely humbled and shamed. I know this journey has been far from easy, and You've made it light for me in recent years, but I just need Your strength more than ever now. I need Your guidance more than ever. I need to know that I've been forgiven and that it's okay to move forward. I need to know that the women and men I've hurt along the way have healed. I need to know if there are any loose ends I need to tie up. I need to know if any of my brothers and sisters have an alt against me that I'm unaware of."

The timer on the dryer went off, but I continued praying, "Lord, I need to be able to discern, going forward, how to address *everybody*. If there's someone hurting beside me, help me to recognize it. If there's someone who needs help or a shoulder to lean on, help me to give me them the right words to say. Help me to encourage them, not turn them away. Help me to be an example of the life YOU lived, Lord," I prayed, feeling a stream of warm tears flowing down my face.

"Lord, I just thank You for saving me. I thank You for giving me other chances to get this thing right. I've fallen hundreds of times and still You love me. Still, You've kept me. Still, You've proven to me Your unfailing love. I give You all the glory for never giving up on me even in my mess-ups and sins. I thank You even now for my daughters, and for protecting us all with all the madness that's going on."

The words and sincerity flowed from my lips like water. I was unstoppable as I addressed my heavenly father.

"I pray for Marisha—wherever she is, and whatever state of mind she's in. I pray for her safety. May she stay sane and may You keep her. I pray that she doesn't do anything that could cause harm to herself or others. I also ask that You would just give her peace and to walk in forgiveness."

I wiped my face and looked towards the ceiling, finally opening my eyes. More fresh tears left my eyes. "I'm sorry for all that I've done. I can't say it enough. I'm sorry for my actions that have brought consequences, fears, and negativity to my family. Please continue to fix this messed up life of mine and guide me so that I never turn back to my wicked ways. Help me to be a better father and a better disciple. In Your name, I pray. Amen."

As the final words of my prayer hit the atmosphere, I felt an indescribable peace that could not be explained or contained. I smiled, immediately knowing that God had answered my prayers and given me concord. My heart no longer raced with heartache and panic, but there was a settling in my spirit. I kissed my folded hands and then aimed them upward, thanking God one final time before I left out of the laundry room. As I opened the door, both Summer and Autumn fell into the room.

I could do nothing but chuckle weakly as I embraced them. Clearly, they had heard everything, but at that point, I didn't care. I needed them to know their old man would be okay. No words were said, and it seemed to be understood that God had us. We didn't need to worry or have any fears for the future because all was going to be well. I gave them each a kiss on the forehead, and then walked them to the living room where we sat and ate a simple dinner of frozen pizza and crinkle cut fries.

Chapter Fifteen

(One week later)

I could not believe I was standing in the funeral home that housed Kyla's body. From the moment I pulled up and parked, to the time that I made my way inside, I could feel heaviness in my spirit. It weighed on the back of my neck, traveled through my heart, and down to my toes. Wherever I stepped and went, it followed. Seeing all of the solemn staff members, smelling the pungency of fresh flowers, and witnessing Kyla's upset family members and loved ones added to the emotional pain I already felt.

I thought about everything I'd been taught about life and death. Before Jesus came as a baby to the world and lived and died for the sins of mankind, there was Adam and Eve, the first humans to ever walk and enjoy the earth. After their fall from grace and the eating of the forbidden fruit, death became inevitable for *everyone*. So, for Christians, death had no sting, or at least it shouldn't have. This was especially true when you knew where a person was headed in the afterlife. Heaven and hell were very real places, and I wasn't sure if Kyla had accepted Jesus as her personal Savior before passing away, but I prayed she did for the sake of her soul. Still, any death was sad because it was the reality that our loved ones would no longer be seen or heard again in the physical sense.

I broke free from my thoughts and took a deep exhale.

"God, please help the family through this calamity. Be a comforter," I prayed aloud, adjusting my bowtie and straightening the back of my suit jacket. I stepped further inside, peering around to make sure I was in the right place. I saw Kyla's name on one of the doors and went inside to view her body for the final time.

My breath caught in my throat as I immediately noticed Kyla with her arms wrapped around a fetus. Kyla must have gone into labor posthumously, and the funeral home thought it was appropriate to display the baby's tiny body. The baby even wore a tiny dress and favored a doll almost. The surreal presence of the deceased baby brought on tears that I had no idea was at bay. Lying in the cream-colored casket were hopes and dreams, promising futures, and beautiful lives cut way too short. I figured I had done all of my crying, but I was mistaken as I hurriedly wiped my sleeve across my eyes and cleared my throat. If not for anyone else, I had to be strong for the family who looked on.

I grabbed an obituary and walked further up to the front to get a better view. I was about to stand directly before Kyla's body to bid her a goodbye when a finger tapped my shoulder. I turned and looked down at the small, fragile looking woman who was dressed in her Sunday's best. She was shaped like a pear, and wrinkles of wisdom adorned her face. Grief shone through her big, brown eyes. The loose, aging skin around her eyes, cheeks, and neck did not take away from her natural beauty. She favored Kyla, so I figured it must have been her grandmother.

"I saw you on the news. You're the young man who was there the night my grandbaby died," she whispered, patting my cheeks and smiling weakly. Three missing teeth were revealed. "I'm sure you tried to save her, and the family thanks you. We know you did all you could."

"I tried, ma'am. I really did. Your granddaughter was a friend of mine and I cared for her. I'm so sorry for your loss," I told her sincerely, catching another tear as it made its way down my cheek. "If you all need anything, please call me."

"Write down your number for me, baby."

I did as told, and then kissed the sweet woman on her forehead. She settled in a seat at the front, removed her hat, and then proceeded to fan herself with one of the obituaries. I could hear her begin to hum an old hymn as she comforted herself.

I walked back over to Kyla's side, kissed my fingers, and then touched those same fingers to her cool, stiff hand. She did not look like she'd been shot to death. She looked peaceful. Her make up was done exquisitely, and she was wearing a normal colored wig for a change. I could not do anything but chuckle that even in death, she was fashionable. There was even a bit of a smirk on her face. Perhaps an angel was entertaining her in the spiritual realm.

"Until we meet again, Ky."

I knew I didn't have the strength to stay through her funeral, so I said my final goodbye, and turned on my black dress shoes to walk out.

As I reached the car, and began to get in, someone ran up on the side of me.

"Jalen Owens! Sir…can we have a word with you?"

I peered over my shoulder at the camera crew that had cornered me. *Not this again*, I thought, and closed my door shut, leaning against it.

The reporter did not wait for a reply, and began to film and ask me questions. "This is Alexander Wilcox from Channel 9 News. We're here at the funeral of the slain young woman, who, along with her unborn baby, lost their lives over a week ago by her jealous ex-husband. That night, you were there. Can you tell us how you're feeling in this moment?"

I stared at the man in disbelief. "You said it yourself. We're at her FUNERAL. How else do you expect me to feel? She was a woman with hopes, dreams, and had a baby on the way. She was a woman with accomplishments under her belt and a business that she ran with love and pride. She was a person…somebody's daughter, sister, cousin, and friend. I'm sad…I'm heartbroken…just as the rest of her family and friends are."

"Again, we're very sorry for your loss. How have you been recovering from that night? Is it true that you were also shot?"

"I was never shot, just roughened up. What's the point of this interview?"

"We understand your frustrations, but we just wanted to update the community. Have you heard anything more about the gunman or any charges? We spoke to the police department this morning and they declined to comment."

I gritted my teeth as I turned to open the car door again. "That's exactly what I'm doing now. With all due respect, on all days, can you just give it a rest? There are people mourning and entering this funeral home to see their loved one for the last time. She was more than a news topic. Let the people grieve in peace!"

The news reporter saw that he wasn't going to get much more out of me and motioned for his cameraman to cease filming. "Sir, we apologize for the…"

I sat in my car and slammed the door, cutting off his words. I gripped the steering wheel in anger and yelled out to myself. Then I slammed my palms against the leather as hard as I could. I didn't want to do any interviews or answer any questions anymore. I didn't want to receive random phone calls from news stations that wanted the latest scoop on what was going on. I didn't even want to have to testify on Leonard in the coming months, but it was now my reality.

I yelled out again, nearly shaking my car in the process at the force. Whether I had an audience or not, the outburst was needed and made me feel a little bit better. The guilt that I felt from not being able to save Kyla wasn't going anywhere anytime soon, but for the moment I felt relieved.

"Honey, may I help you?" An older biracial woman questioned me as I entered Parkway Townhomes in search of Alani.

As crazy as it sounded, all throughout the day and even during Kyla's viewing, I had been thinking about Alani, and just needed to see her. Each time we'd talked over the phone or in person, there was a certain peace she exuded, and I had to follow through with my gut feeling that told me to go to the local grocery store, buy a couple of items, and head her way. The girls were excited to see our future home again, but I told them to stay in the car for now. I didn't plan to stay here long. I merely wanted to make Alani smile and leave her guessing until our move-in day.

I looked over and jumped slightly at the imposing voice. The woman's deep auburn hair was thick and flowed like satin around her shoulders. Her cinnamon-colored skin had the most beautiful freckles sprinkled about and she wore wore-rimmed glasses that did her hazel eyes no justice. To be an older woman, she was very shapely and well put together and smelled like warm vanilla.

For the first time in my life, I blushed under the gaze of a woman. "Yes, I was looking for...um..."

"The property manager?" she finished my thought.

"Yes, I...we...um..."

The woman chuckled as she continued to lock up the office while swinging a large purse over her shoulder. "Cat got your tongue, honey? Alani went home early today, though. She wasn't feeling well. Are you looking to schedule an appointment for a showing or here to drop off rent?"

"Neither. I…um…" I stuttered. "I've already signed an upcoming lease and will be staying here for the next year."

"Then just why are you here, young man, and dressed so nicely, might I add?" the woman prodded, gently resting her weight from one foot to the next. She continued to stare me down with those striking eyes.

"Honestly? I was bringing her boxed chocolates and a rose for all of the help and guidance she gave me in the process of finding this place. That's all. I was a fool to mix business with my personal affairs anyway, so I'll be leaving. Plus, my twins are waiting in the car for me," I rushed to say, spinning around to leave, but before I could walk away, she spun me back around.

The woman smiled empathetically, perusing me from my head to my toes. Again, I could not help blushing under her intense stare. Finally, after pulling her glasses off the bridge of her nose and tucking them in the neckline of her blouse, she motioned with her head for me to follow her.

"Come this way, sweetheart."

I followed her, not understanding where she was taking me, but somehow trusting her kind smile. She led me outside and down a short block of townhomes where television programs and light chatter could be heard with every passing door. We came to a home in particular that had a beautiful welcome mat in front, and a scripture decal on the wooden door. *"As for me and my house, we will serve the Lord,"* it read.

The woman knocked twice and then stood back. She winked at me while I waited nervously for who was coming to the door.

"I'm Helena, by the way."

"Jalen." We shook hands.

The person took their time coming to the door because more than a minute had passed before the door opened leisurely.

To my surprise and delight, Alani stood before us, dressed in a camisole and pajama shorts with a leopard print scarf around her head, and thick socks on her feet. She looked awful as she stared at the woman who had led me this way.

"Hey, Momma. Come on in. Excuse the tissues on the floor."

My eyes nearly popped out of my head at the realization. No wonder Alani was so gorgeous and charming. She had certainly gotten her looks and personality from her mother. They looked more like sisters than mother and daughter.

"Baby, you also have a guest," Helena pointed out, clearing her throat.

Alani looked over and gasped suddenly, rushing to hide from me. I couldn't help but to chuckle under my breath. Despite her sickness, she still wanted to look presentable for me. Yet I found her breathtaking even with her raspy voice, reddened nose, and flushed cheeks.

"Oh, my goodness. I didn't even see you there. Jalen...what...what are you doing here? Mom, why didn't you warn me?" She rushed to remove her scarf and finger-combed through her hair.

"I just did. Girl, relax. You look fine...*sick*, but fine." Helena pushed past her daughter, sauntering towards the kitchen and making herself right at home.

"Thanks *a lot*, Mother," she said sarcastically, eyeing Helena with a hint of embarrassment and annoyance.

"I'm sorry for imposing. I just wanted to bring you a little thank you gift for all of your help. Me and the girls really appreciate you."

Her eyes softened as I broke off the stem of the rose and tucked it behind her ear. Then I placed the boxed chocolates in her petite hands.

"I hope you're not allergic," I added.

"No, no. These are my favorites. Thank you so much. You didn't have to do this, but I truly thank you for making my day."

"Jalen, honey, are you hungry?" Helen called out. The clanging of pots and pans could be heard. "I'm making my baby girl some dinner and can always make enough for five people."

"Five? Oh! Are your girls here too?"

"Yeah, I left them in the car. It's okay, really, I just wanted to drop these things off and..."

"It's settled! Alani, go freshen up while I start on the food. Jalen, go grab your daughters from the car. The door will be unlocked when you return."

"Are you positive? You look like you need rest, not company," I told Alani.

"This woman is relentless," she chuckled. "You can stay if you'd like, but it's no pressure. I won't feel bad."

Less than an hour later, we were saying grace over the food and digging in with watery mouths. Helena was an amazing cook and had made a mini Thanksgiving feast, including mustard greens, baked chicken breasts and gravy, macaroni and cheese, and hot water cornbread. Apparently, Friday evenings were their mother-daughter nights where they cooked and spent time with one another. Alani normally went to her mother's house, but because she was sick, Helena insisted she do the running around.

Helena and her ex-husband, Alani's father, were the building owners while Alani served as the property manager. I felt even better knowing it was a family business and looked forward to my stay at the townhomes. The girls took to both women well and seemed to be enjoying themselves as they ate seconds. Helena eventually brought out a tub of ice cream and purposely summoned the girls to the downstairs den where they put on a movie.

Alani smiled shyly as the room grew quiet. "My mom is something else."

"She's incredible."

"Thank you. I don't know what I'd do without her." Alani stood and began to clear the table of dirty dishes and utensils, but I touched her arm and ordered her to sit back down.

"Have a seat. I'll clean them for you. The girls say I wash the dishes well."

"I was just going to place them in the dishwasher," she teased, sitting back down.

"Well, I'll be the best dishwasher user you've ever seen," I countered back playfully, gathering up the soiled napkins and empty water bottles.

She laughed and watched me navigate around her kitchen. "Did you enjoy dinner?"

"Oh, yeah. It was nice to get a good hearty meal like that. Me and the girls were just wondering, on the way over, what we were going to eat."

"I'm glad. Mom can throw down. I taught her a few things."

"Is that right?" I chuckled.

"She's lying! I taught her everything *she* knows!" Helena shouted out playfully, coming up the stairs. She placed the tub of ice cream back into the freezer, winked at us, and then walked back out without another word.

We both shared a laugh as we looked at one another.

"Thanks for putting those dishes away. Now come sit. I'm the sick one, but you look exhausted. Is everything okay?" Alani questioned, watching me under thick, curly eyelashes. She tucked her legs under her and wrapped herself in a blanket while she studied me. As I sat down, she tucked the blanket around me too.

"I'm okay. There's just been a lot going on. Nothing that a little prayer and perseverance won't do."

"Speaking of which, I saw the news coverage about you saving lives and holding a gunman down. What in the world happened with that?"

181

I gave a weak smile. "It's a very long story, and one that may keep you up at night if you knew *all* the details. But long story short, I was having dinner with an ex-girlfriend, and her husband showed up and pulled out a gun. He ended up killing her, but when he moved to shoot me, his gun jammed and that's when my survival mode kicked in."

"Your ex-girlfriend's husband? What?" Alani leaned in as if it was good gossip that she was hearing. "How long ago did you guys date? I'm so sorry to hear that. The news report also said that she was pregnant. Is that true?"

I swallowed hard, not expecting her to delve deeper into the backstory. "Well, it was…more of a two to three date kind of thing with her, and then we separated. Yes, she was pregnant, and she was planning to leave him, but…well…you know how that ended."

"I don't know how you sleep at night after witnessing that. My God!"

"It was hard, and it's still been hard, but God has given me strength during this time. All I can do is move forward and make sure he's put away for good for her and the baby's sake."

Alani shook her head sadly. "I'm praying for you and her family. I can't imagine."

"Thank you. I needed it more than ever today when I saw her for the last time." I clapped my hands together. "But let's not ruin this evening with all that sad talk. I wanted to ask, and I guess this should have been my first question, but are you seeing anyone?"

"No, I'm not seeing anyone, and haven't been seen for over six years." She smiled. "Don't get me wrong, I'm content with my singleness, but it does get lonely sometimes when all your friends get together and they have spouses and children. Sometimes I wonder, Lord, am I just meant to serve You and be single for a lifetime?"

I watched her grow quiet and peer down at her fingernails that were long and all natural.

"Of course not. There's a man out there hurting for you, trust me."

"*Hurting* for me?" She raised her eyebrows, intrigued.

"Absolutely. He's missing his rib. He has to be in some sort of pain until you two meet."

For a moment, it looked like Alani's eyes glazed over in tears, but she blinked them away and the corners of her mouth lifted into that brilliant smile of hers again.

"That's very sweet of you. Thank you. Now, according to your daughter, there is no Misses *yet* but is there at least a lady in your life?"

I chuckled a bit and watched the muted television. "No. I promised God I wouldn't get involved with any relationship until He says otherwise."

"I can respect that. I'm sure you've had lots of women in your day, you being the all-mighty Pastor Jalen, and all."

Her words caused me to freeze in place. The way she said it was harmless, but then again, I could not be too sure. Her eyes never changed, and her smile never faltered as she waited for a reply.

"You…you know of me?"

"This entire state knows about you, Jalen," she laughed. "I'm sure the entire Midwest knows of you. I knew who you were from the moment you stepped into my office to apply for a home. Will I let that determine what I think of you? Will I let those preconceived opinions and rumors play a part in getting to know you? Absolutely not. I have a past too, you know, so who am I to judge?"

I could appreciate her honesty and her willingness to look past my shortcomings. I sat back and looked at her with mild fascination. "Do tell."

Alani blushed as she looked off into the distance, explaining herself, "I wasn't always saved, sanctified and Holy Ghost filled. I was promiscuous in my younger days. Don't look so shocked."

"College days?"

"Try again." She wrapped herself tighter in the blanket. "I was in high school, trying to prove myself and trying to be grown. Whew, I was a mess, Jalen. By senior year, I can say I'd gone through half the football team. Sad, right? I'd like to think it stemmed from peer pressure and wanting to look like the cool kid, but who knows? With a father who was always working and never there half the time, and a mother who was strung out on drugs at the time, I needed attention. Any attention would do, so I turned to boys."

I was astonished at all the information she was sharing, but grateful. Obviously, she trusted little old me. Helena did not look like she had ever held a cigarette before, much less been addicted to drugs. In the same way, Alani seemed reserved and shy, so to know she was once promiscuous was a shock.

"You were trying to fill a void," I added.

"Exactly. That's exactly it. I know now that I was searching for some sort of happiness, but I thank God I didn't get any diseases or became pregnant along the way. I've had a few heartbreaks, which I needed to experience in order to grow, but overall, I discovered salvation my sophomore year in college and haven't turned back since. Through God, I was healed and have shared my story with a bunch of young ladies who were just like me."

I nodded. "It's the best life anyone can live."

"Yes! I honestly wouldn't trade it for the world."

I got comfortable on the couch, crossing my legs at the ankle. "Your last boyfriend. What was he like?"

"He was my fiancé, and he was controlling. Ugh," Alani shuddered at the thought, her eyes growing darker. "He had serious anger issues. He was a control freak and wanted to know my every move and would get upset when I didn't tell him. I left him before things got too serious or before he put his hands on me. Last I heard, he's married with two children, and I pray for that woman every day. I hope she's not going through what he put me through."

I nodded, listening to her sultry voice that sounded nasally every so often. She stood up to blow her nose and then washed her hands. After drying her hands with paper towel, I watched her squirt a bit of lotion onto her hands, rubbing it in sensually.

"I'm so sorry. This is so unattractive."

"My twins suffer from seasonal allergies, so I understand. It's not unattractive. It's a part of life. You're still easy on the eyes, trust me."

She plopped back down on the couch and turned towards me fully. "Oh, stop. You're just saying that."

"I don't say things I don't mean."

Alani watched me for a moment, not saying anything. It was like she was reading my mind, and perhaps even reading my soul.

185

"Can I be honest with you?"

"You've been honest all night. Why stop now?"

Alani took a deep breath. "I can't believe I'm about to say this, but you know that day I called you about the background check?"

I nodded.

"When I put you on hold, I prayed about you. I prayed for confirmation that I was doing the right thing by overriding those errors on your application, and that I was making the right choice by allowing you to live here."

"And what did God say?"

"Well, it's obvious, right? I approved you. I just wanted you to know that our family welcomes you with open arms, not just at the townhomes, but in general. I know things probably have not been easy, considering all the controversy that has surrounded your name, but just like I wasn't thrown away and forgotten about, neither are you."

"A God-fearing, praying woman. I love it, and you don't know how much that means to me."

"My pleasure. Now, although I would *love* to keep you here all night and talk about you, my head feels like it's going to explode. I would hate for you to catch me with snot running down my face or something worse," she continued, gradually scooting to the edge of the couch. "You know where I live now."

"I do."

"Don't be a stranger."

"Trust me, Ms. Alani, I won't." I grabbed her hand and kissed the back of it. "You have a goodnight, okay? I'm going to pull the car around. Can you gather the girls for me?"

"I will." She smiled.

I headed home with the scent of Alani's hand lotion on my nose, and my head in the clouds—a feeling I hadn't felt in a while.

Chapter Sixteen

With a refreshed mind, I returned to work and moved forward with my life, one day at a time. It was time to buckle down and focus on making money and living life without any more regrets or poor decision-making. I knew the worst was behind me, and the best was yet to come for my family and me. We moved into our new townhome with excitement and pride, and the girls started school two weeks later. I was thrilled to get them back into a healthy social atmosphere with other youth their age. Summer planned to tryout for the cheerleading team, while Autumn wanted to be on Student Council. I couldn't be prouder as a father.

Alani and I grew closer with every conversation we shared, and discovered we had so many things in common. She was the breath of fresh air that I desired and was the perfect balance to my lifestyle. Whereas she grew frantic over the little things, I was calm and laidback. In the moments where I became unorganized and off-task, she gave me the focus I needed. Alani was sweet, centered, and a woman of her word. We were not necessarily looking for love or a relationship, but whatever we had, felt good.

Being with her and around her felt right.

As I prepared for a meeting with a new client, I listened to smooth jazz softly from my computer monitor and looked around to make sure the office looked presentable. Everything was neat and in order, from the plants, to the wall paintings, to the way my papers were stacked in the corner of my desk. The night cleaners had my office spotless, well vacuumed, and dust-free, plus the automatic plug-in air freshener sent off sweet scents every 36 minutes. Surely, my client would feel right at home.

I sighed, feeling butterflies enter my stomach.

"You got this, Jay. You got this," I offered myself a pep talk, drumming my thumbs against the desk.

I looked obsessively at my phone, waiting on the secretary to page me and send the client my way. This new business partner had the potential to give the company a new stream of revenue and added exposure in Corporate America. I wondered why my supervisor thought I was the best candidate to take on such a major partner, but then again, with God, all things were possible. Just like any other challenge, I'd kill this one and come away victorious.

Beeeeep. My eyes darted to the blinking phone. "Hi, Mr. Owens?"

Showtime, I thought.

"Yes, Candy?"

"Your prospective is here, with a few other guests. Shall I gather more chairs from the conference room?"

More guests? I looked around with nervousness, seeing two chairs and a loveseat.

"How many more would you say?"

"Um," she could be heard counting faintly. "Seven total people are here."

My heart dropped completely, jumping to my feet in slight panic. I looked in the small mirror that was stationed inside of my closet and made sure there was no food in my teeth, crust in my eyes, or ash on my face. I adjusted my clothing, breathed in and out deeply, and then closed the door to my closet.

189

Just before leaving out of the office, Candy paged me once more. "Oh, Mr. Owens? Are you still there?"

"Yes, I was heading out now," I called out to her. "Is something wrong?"

"I'm sorry. No, nothing's wrong," her voice was high-pitched and drenched with excitement as she spoke. "Oh, my goodness. This isn't your prospective client. It's someone *major*, Mr. Owens!"

Alani

"Give me two more minutes and we're done, ladies!" The middle-aged instructor shouted at me and 18 other women as we nearly hit the 60-minute mark of cycling class. She spoke through her small headset, which allowed her chipper voice to permeate the fitness studio. I didn't necessarily care for her voice, but it proved to be motivational in this moment as I gritted my teeth and gave the bicycle all I had.

I'm sure I wasn't the only woman whose calf muscles and buttocks screamed out with soreness. The entire class had been alternating between sitting and standing on our stationary bikes. I hated and loved the burn all the same, because it meant that my summer body for next year was underway. I wanted to be ahead of the game and shed a few more pounds before the winter holidays in the meantime.

"Come on. One minute remaining!" the instructor continued, walking around and admiring us all. She pumped her fists to the hip hop music blaring overhead. Homegirl had a little soul in her. "Let's get it, ladies!"

I leaned forward on the bicycle, my elbows tucked in the handlebars, and puffs of breath leaving my mouth sporadically. I was dripping from head to toe in sweat and my purple and black active gear clung to my body like a second skin. A towel was thrown around my neck, catching a few droplets that left my forehead and nose. Today's workout had gotten the best of me, but I felt good.

"Whew! Good job, girls! I'll see you at the same time and same place next week."

I waved a goodbye to a few of my workout buddies while I settled on a yoga mat, feeling sore but amazing. I was down 14 pounds from the class alone and planned to keep up with it until I lost my goal of 30 total pounds.

In the wall-to-wall mirror, I did a quick stretch of my limbs and torso on the mat, and then jumped to my feet. Now that my morning fitness was out of the way, I needed to run a few errands and pick up a few things for the house. I made sure I looked halfway presentable by finger-combing my hair to the back of my head and throwing a windbreaker over my arms to cover up the sweat spots that had seeped through my clothes.

As I crossed the street and headed for my car, I could hear someone whistling. *Really?* I thought, continuing to walk and feeling annoyed at the catcall. It was 2018, for crying out loud, and you'd think men knew how to approach women by now. I shook my head and took the key fob out, unlocking my car doors. The whistling grew more aggressive and closer but still, my instincts told me to face forward and keep calm. As I reached to open the door of my navy blue four-seater, that I'd bought myself over two years ago, another hand reached out and closed around my wrist. I screamed in panic, choosing to react *first* and ask questions *later*.

Sick of the shenanigans, I took out my small can of mace and sprayed my would-be assailant. He yelled out in agony as pepper spray met his eyes. I turned fully to face the man who had snuck up on me, shocked to find that I knew my attacker all along.

"Tony, is that you?" I coughed and peered through the red haze down at the flailing arms and legs. "Tony, what is wrong with you, sneaking up on me?"

I watched my ex-fiancé struggle to breathe and compose himself, as he wiped frantically at his fiery red eyes. Nothing seemed to give him relief as he took his shirt off and rubbed his eyes with it. I felt halfway bad, watching as he rolled around on the ground, in the middle of the street. The other part of me felt a bit of satisfaction that he was in pain. It was no match to what he had put me through in our previous relationship, I'm sure.

"Dang, girl! I was just being funny. I saw you coming out of the studio while I was at the bank and wanted to surprise you."

"I never liked surprises, and you know that," I told him, leaning down and offering a hand. "I'm sorry for spraying you, but I thought you were attacking me."

Once upon a time, I was in love with this former college basketball star who stood at 6'5," with muscles for days, a baldhead, and just the right amount of bad boy in him. Anthony Grady was the total package and everything a woman could have prayed for. He had an excellent job with benefits, drove a car that most men wanted and most women admired, owned his home, and took care of his sickly mother like any good man should. Without any children or a girlfriend at the time, I'd practically fallen into his arms after only a few dates. He wooed me and showed me the finer things in life, but it was his attitude and possessive personality that caused us to separate.

He ended up being no good for me, and I was happy to move on if it meant keeping my joy and sanity intact. I had not seen Anthony in awhile and wondered why he chose today, of all days, to meet up with me. If my memory served me correctly, it was the same day we called off our engagement so many years ago.

Anthony was finally able to get himself together and get his vision under control, and although his eyes were now bloodshot and sticky, he could at least look me in the eye. Tears streamed down his face as he looked at me sideways. "I swear that was my first and last time ever sneaking up on you. Dang! I can't believe you sprayed me, Lani."

"I'm sorry." I suppressed a smile and took a step back onto the curb, away from the oncoming traffic. "You okay? I have bottled water that you can use to flush out your eyes."

He sniffed and then wiped his face a final time with the back of his hand. "Nah, I should be okay. You didn't get me too bad. How are you doing otherwise? You still look good."

"Thanks." I offered an unsure smile. "What are you doing here?"

"Like I said, I was in the bank across the

street when I saw you coming out. So, I ran over to say hello."

"Of all days, huh? You somehow found your way to me on the 27th of September, huh?"

Anthony looked at his wristwatch as if he didn't realize the day's date. He lifted his eyebrows and feigned surprise. "Oh, for real? I didn't even remember what today was. That's craaazy."

"Tony, stop playing. You called me a month ago while I was at work. You sent me flowers two weeks ago, and now you mysteriously show back up in my life on the day we broke off our engagement. What's going on? Don't insult my intelligence or waste any more of my time. I have things to do, you know."

"I realize that, girl. I know you've got your family business to run, and all that good stuff. I'm proud of you. I'm not trying to waste your time."

I pressed my lips together and looked him up and down. He was dressed comfortably in athleisure gear. I remember us being that "faithfully fit" couple that ran together *every* morning before work and then somehow ending up kissing passionately with a lake or park as our backdrop. We would go to work late *many* times, unable to contain our excitement for each other as we parted ways. Those morning runs were some of the highlights of our relationship.

"Then, just what are you doing? As I recall, you have a wife and child, right? Or is it two now? How's the family doing?"

Anthony grimaced as I threw everything I'd learned about him in his face. It had been a while since we talked, but I at least knew he had moved on. Dating and starting over in another relationship with another man was something I could not see myself doing just yet. However, as my mind drifted to Jalen, I knew it could be sooner than later. There was just something about him that spoke to my soul.

We were just as much alike as we were different, and he made life fun for me again. Although we only saw each other a few times since his initial surprise visit, I often found myself thinking, *what if?* What if we were destined to be together? What if God had perfectly orchestrated our love stories to intertwine? I had no desires to open my heart ever again to anyone, but if the moment was right, Jalen was a perfect candidate.

Anthony snapped his fingers, freeing me from my daydream. "Okay, let's cut right to it since you know me from the inside-out. I'm not even going to lie. The day you broke up with me, I didn't care if we ever saw each other again. You didn't like the direction our relationship was going, and that was fine with me. But as time has passed, and I've married my dream girl and had a couple beautiful children, I realize this is the life I've always wanted."

"So, what exactly is the problem?" I took a sip of my water and dabbed my face with my towel. "You literally have it all."

"It's the life I've always wanted for you and I."

"You can't be serious, Tony," I whispered, tossing his nickname in the atmosphere again. "Don't…don't do this."

"I want you back, Lani," he added softly, reaching out and cupping my face in his hands. "I have a speaking engagement tonight and was hoping you could accompany me. I'm sure you'll be the prettiest face in the building."

I jerked away from his touch, feeling

disgusted.

"No! No...you don't have the right to just come back into my life and demand something like that! First of all, you have a WIFE...and children, Anthony! What kind of man are you to play those kinds of games? And who do you think I am to take you back and to be a side chick? Boy, that mace must've gotten to your head! Who do you think you are?"

His face was intense with emotion, while he patted his chest where his heart was. "An unhappy man who recognizes who his *true* love is."

"But that's just it. I've moved forward. I don't love you anymore. It's the same as the day we broke up. You were not the one for me then, and you aren't the one for me now. I'm sorry to sound so harsh, but it's the truth, Tony. We cannot and will not be together," I explained, feeling warm tears rush to my eyes.

I was not necessarily hurt or confused by the situation, but I felt bad for his wife who was clueless right now while her husband pursued another woman. What kind of fool did Anthony think I was?

"So, you're telling me that you haven't revisited the idea of us together? You're completely done with *us*? Is that what you're saying to me?" Anthony asked, looking around at onlookers as he professed his love. "Alani, I LOVE you...and have never loved another woman since."

"As cold as it sounds," I began, rounding my car and reaching for the handle. "No. I'm not in love with you, and I have not revisited the idea of us getting back together. We just weren't right for each other, Tony. Please understand that I'm happy right where I am."

We stared at each other for what seemed

like an eternity, but it was only a couple of seconds. His dark eyes stayed with me as he nodded, and then he backed away slightly. He held up his hands, forcing a smile my way.

"Wow. I can see it in your eyes how serious you are. Is there another man in the picture?"

"I do care for someone else, yes, but…in general, I'm content with my singleness right now. God has done some amazing things in my life, and I'm just trying to serve Him and get myself ready for where He's taking me. That's all."

"I'm…I'm sorry for disrupting your life," he stuttered.

"You don't have to be sorry. Good luck with your engagement tonight, and you take care, you hear?"

"You too, Alani. You too." Anthony stepped onto the curb and watched me settle in my car. He placed his hand on the window and only lifted his hand when I pulled off down the street.

I drove away with the pitiful image of Anthony in my rearview mirror and headed home, no longer motivated to run errands or do anything productive. All I wanted was a few large scoops of fudge and brownie pieces ice cream and to curl up on my couch. As I pulled into my complex, I passed by Jalen's unit and smiled instinctively. My happiness and the butterflies I felt could not be contained whenever we were near each other. In this case, he had no idea how much better he made my day just by passing by his home.

In tune with my thoughts, I could feel my phone buzz as Jalen's number popped up along with a picture of him and the girls that I'd taken during our last outing.

"Hello? You must have seen me passing by."

"No, I'm not home. I'm actually out shopping for a tuxedo."

"Oh! A tuxedo? What is it for, a church function?" I pulled into my garage and got out, enjoying the smoothness of his voice in my ear. His voice seemed to ease away the day's frustrations and stress.

"Alani, you won't believe what happened. Today, the mayor and his personal assistant stopped by my office today and invited me to the city's 10th Annual Mayoral Black and White Ball. I'm the recipient of an award for my efforts that night of the shooting."

"What? Are you serious?" I paused while entering the side entrance of my home. "That's amazing. Congratulations."

"They apologized for the short notice, and understood if I couldn't make it, but this is something I couldn't pass up. My boss let me off early so I could find something nice to wear."

"I'm so proud of you. This is *your* moment," I encouraged him, sitting my keys on the countertop. I headed to my bedroom where I kicked off my shoes and began to undress while balancing the phone between my shoulder and ear.

"Thank you, sweetheart. That means a lot. Give me a second, okay?" Jalen grew quiet as I heard the beeps of his items being scanned and purchased in the background. "Okay, I'm back. So, you know I have to ask."

I leaned over the tub, running water for a bath. It filled up quickly as I waited for him to continue his thought. "What's that?"

"I can bring another person with me, and you immediately came to mind. I know it's super last minute, but if you're free, I would love to have you on my arm."

I added bubbles and a bath bomb to the water, easing in. I put the phone on speaker and slid down until my chin touched the surface of the water. "I wouldn't miss it for the world," I confessed, closing my eyes. "What time should I be ready?"

"Give me an hour."

"I got you."

We talked a moment more and then hung up from one another.

Chapter Seventeen

After my relaxing, 17-minute bath, I dried off and moisturized my body from head to toe. I had never attended any kind of ball, other than the few fancy-schmancy gatherings that Anthony would take me to, so I had no idea how dressy to get. I decided on a white dress that hung to my ankles. It accentuated my slimmer waistline beautifully, and was off the shoulder, baring one of my toned arms.

The dress was super conservative from the front, but with every stride in my five-inch heels, a thigh-high split was revealed along with my golden skin beneath. I hoped it wasn't too overboard; I didn't want to give off the wrong impression or show Jalen a different side of me, but I figured it was okay to be both classy and sexy for his big night.

Usually, my hair would be my biggest problem on any given day, but tonight, it submitted to my comb and brush like a well-trained child. I pulled my hair completely back, and then rolled it into a French twist, pinning it with bobby pins and sealing it with a little spray. With my pinkies, I pulled out a few wisps of hair to frame my face. Natural looking makeup and gold jewelry completed my look along with a few squirts of perfume. As I stepped into the living room where Jalen had entered minutes before, I was met with his strong back.

He looked totally in control of the night and wore his black, velvet tuxedo like a groom on his wedding day. From head to toe, he was sharp, fitted, and tailored to perfection. His hair was freshly cut, and his facial hair was trimmed up nicely. His muscles could be seen through the material of his clothes, and whiffs of his cologne nearly brought me to my knees. He was extra sexy as he peered out of the window, and exuded confidence like no other while he shoved his hands in his pockets. I watched him for a moment more before clearing my throat. Jalen turned around with a smile, but it soon dropped when our eyes met.

"Is…something wrong?" I asked, biting my lip shyly. I could not read the look on his face.

"*Alani,*" he whispered, as though I took his breath away. He looked at me as if I was the most beautiful woman in the world. "Wow."

I took his speechlessness as a compliment and blushed, bowing my head. He walked over briskly and took my hands in his, drinking up my presence with his eyes.

"You look amazing. I'm so lucky to be your date tonight," he crooned.

"As I am yours."

"Can I…?" Jalen began to ask, and then shook his head. "Never mind."

"Yes, you may kiss me," I completed his thought, touching my hand to his face.

He did not need any further encouragement as he wrapped me in his arms and picked me up off of the floor. I gasped before his lips claimed mine in a sensual dance. We kissed for a minute or two, until I was sure that my lipstick was gone, and his lips were swollen. We pulled away from one another, and he placed me back on solid ground. I felt dizzy but in a good way. We kissed once more before smiling at each other. Sparks flew between us as we held hands and made our way outside in the cool evening.

We headed to the car with his hand on my lower back and like a gentleman, he helped me into the car. From the time that we left, to the moment we arrived at the coliseum, Jalen held my hand in his and kept an eye on me as if he was scared that I'd disappear if he looked away. I could not help but to appreciate the way he made me feel. The way he treated me put my head in the clouds, and I did not want to come down.

I felt like a woman...*his* woman.

We made our way inside but not before walking a red carpet and talking to a few members of the local media and news outlets. Jalen spoke articulately and with passion about his friend, Kyla, and the events of the night that he took down the gunman. He reiterated to everyone that he wanted her death to raise awareness for domestic violence, and he spoke on how his faith and belief in God played a major part in saving his life that night. I could tell that he was finally at peace about the situation because he did not grow emotional as he spoke. Instead, he honored her memory in a beautiful way, and encouraged people to hold onto their faith in such troubling times.

All throughout the night, I could not help but smile and glow with pride. We had not known each other long, but I knew of Jalen for many years. This night was his redemption and his time to reclaim the integrity and reputation that had been tarnished long ago. People no longer were talking about his scandals and downfall but were now celebrating his heroic actions and selflessness.

Midway through the ceremony, I excused myself from our table to go to the ladies' room. Jalen kissed my cheek and told me to hurry back because his award presentation was coming up next.

I winked and sauntered off, looking for the restrooms. I found one, did my business, and then washed my hands. I reapplied a bit of powder on my nose and cheeks, and then decided I'd spent enough time away. I could not miss his once in a lifetime opportunity, plus I wanted to record the moment and take lots of pictures. As I walked back out to the table near the front, I was whisked away by a strong arm.

"I can't believe you made it here tonight, and looking lovely, might I add."

For the second time today, I was met with my ex-fiancé's puppy dog eyes. "I didn't come here for you. I didn't even know you were going to be here. Let me go…NOW!"

Anthony looked annoyed but did not follow my instructions. "Then why are you here at *my* function?"

"*Your* function? This is the mayor's ball," I clarified.

"Bingo! Oh! You didn't know I was head secretary to the mayor?"

My eyes nearly popped out of my head. I last knew Anthony to be working for the Board of Trustees for the city but did not know he had climbed the ranks in such a way.

"The man of the hour, Jalen Owens, is my date," I announced proudly, still trying to wean myself away. "And he's probably looking for me. Would you stop it? People are beginning to look."

"Then let them look. You are mighty stunning tonight, baby. Oh! There's my personal photographer. Smile," he said quickly, before a few flashes went off in our faces.

"Give her a kiss!" one of the men shouted, angling his camera to get the perfect view.

"Oh, no you don't!" I hissed, leaning back but unable to stop Anthony's lips from pressing against mine in a forced kiss. More flashes went off and a few people *oohed* and *aahed*.

I blinked to rid my eyes of the blinding flashes and then hit his chest roughly. With anger and repulsion, I wiped my lips and looked at him like he had three eyes. "Are you crazy? Anthony, just STOP! I thought I made it clear earlier that I didn't want you! Why did you do that, like we're some couple in love?"

"If I had my way…" he teased, finally letting me go.

I stumbled slightly from Anthony and into another body. Picking the bottom of my dress from the floor and twirling around, I offered an apologetic and embarrassed smile. "Oops! I'm so sorr—"

My words trailed off as I noticed Jalen was the body I'd bumped into. He stood before me with a disappointed expression on his face and one trembling hand that soon curled into a fist. In the other hand was a silver-tone plaque and certificate that I'd failed to see him receive. He looked at me with hatred in his eyes and appeared like he could hit me right then and there, but I knew he wouldn't.

He did not have to say anything—his face said it all.

I swallowed the lump in my throat. It felt like I'd consumed a spoonful of cinnamon and sugar. In other words, I couldn't breathe. "Listen, Jay, that was…"

"That was the same guy that invited me here, Alani. So, all this time you knew who he was and didn't mention anything? No, no, correction: you were with this man all this time, but then you

204

want to tell me in private how you're single and loving it? I thought you were past those promiscuous days, Alani? Looks to me like you're still flaunting your body around and playing mind games with different men. On my night, of all nights, you want to pull this? You knew how special this night was to me and you played me like that?" Jalen's voice crackled as he stepped back.

"Jalen, *listen*! It's not even like that. I wasn't playing you or lying to you. We're not together! That was my…"

"That was *my* cue to leave. Find you a ride home," he told me, staring at me coldly and then brushing past me.

I watched him push through people and head directly for the door. With my tall heels, it was impossible to keep up as I called his name and tried to ignore the looks I received. In the midst of the crowd of black and white bodies, I saw Anthony standing off to the side with a satisfied smirk on his face. He had done it on purpose—he knew I had come to the event with Jalen, and had done his best to ensure we left separated. He had made me out to look like a complete fool in front of the community and in front of the man I cared for deeply.

Tears surged forward as I finally made it outside where it was pouring raining and there was no Jalen in sight. Lightning struck in the distance and thunder clapped, matching my mood. I knew Jalen was angry, but I knew that I was innocent. I simply needed to explain myself and my history with Anthony. There was no way I was going to let Jalen go to bed tonight with those thoughts in his head that I'd cheated on him or tried to play him. He had to believe me…it was my only hope.

But four hours later, after catching a ride

home, and knocking repeatedly on Jalen's door for an hour only to receive silence and a closed door, I knew I'd messed up badly. Drenched and barefoot, and with my hair and dress plastered to my face and body from the rain, I made my way to my home and collapsed on the couch to cry.

What started off as the perfect night and the beginning of a possible relationship had turned into humiliation, sadness, and to my surprise, a broken heart.

Epilogue

Jalen

There was no way I should have felt the way I did. Following the night of the ball, I went into a sort of depression. I know no woman should have had that effect on me, and especially considering we weren't even official, but I felt some kind of way seeing Alani kiss up on some guy. To make matters worse, she had just kissed me hours before.

What was most disappointing is I thought we had something special, but I guess I didn't know her like I thought I did. Perhaps it was best that we parted ways early on when our feelings weren't so attached. Yet every day that I woke up or went to bed, Alani was on my mind and in my heart. She had done something to me in the short time that we'd gotten to know each other, and it was going to be a long time before I got over her.

Like a fool, I wondered what she was doing and what she was thinking. I wondered if she had cooked or ordered takeout. I wondered what perfume she was wearing, and even wondered if she needed lunch during the workday. What was wrong with me? The woman had downright disrespected and played me—and *publicly* at that, but I was still concerned with her every move. I shook my head as I swam around in the pool that was just off from the community room, willing the thoughts away.

Was I in love? Before that night, did I see myself as more than a friend with Alani? *Absolutely*. I often asked God to reveal Himself when my future wife walked into my life, and she had been a permanent fixture since then. It was a no-brainer that I had fallen for Alani, but somehow, her heart did not align with mine. Maybe she was the one but not in this particular season. All I knew was that I wanted to get my heart and head back, but Alani had them in her clutches.

I couldn't help but to feel nauseous as I thought about the upcoming weeks, months, and years without no longer hearing from Alani. I needed her support as I closed out my final dealings with Marisha, who had been caught sleeping in her car just outside of Arizona. She was arrested, charged, and sent back to Illinois to serve time. On top of that, I would have to not only testify against her, but also Leonard. I felt drained just thinking about the emotional toll even now.

My daughters were good to talk to, but I wouldn't dare share some of the details of what was going on. I had to protect their innocence and keep them children as long as possible. I needed Alani more than ever but didn't want her after what she'd done to me. Who was I kidding? I needed, wanted, and longed for her…*still*…

"Jay, you're a fool. Forget that girl," I told myself.

It was almost midnight and nearing the time that the pool would be closed, but I needed to clear my head a moment more before that time came. I sank down to the bottom of the pool and then came up. I did that a few more times, lingering a little longer each time. As I surfaced after about a minute, I yelled out in shock as I noticed Alani standing before me in a bathing suit.

"You scared me," I told her, pushing water from my eyes.

I shook my face clean of the chlorine-filled

water and stared, unable to look away. Her body was toned and beautiful, and her face was unreadable as she looked at me. The light around the pool gave her an indescribable glow. I should have scoffed at her presence, but I couldn't. Admittedly, she was stunning.

"Can I join?" she asked, sticking one of her feet in and testing the cool water.

"This is a free amenity with our home. You can do whatever you want," I told her, swimming to the opposite side of the pool and as far away from her as possible. Still, I smelled her perfume and the scent of her freshly washed hair. It made my insides jump.

"Really, Jay? Why'd you move so far?"

"We don't need to be close to have a conversation." I attempted to sound as stern as possible, but it sounded more like a child throwing a tantrum.

She sighed, sensing my impatience, and sat down on the edge of the pool. "Can we *please* talk? You've been avoiding my calls and texts."

"How did you know I was here?"

"I didn't. I just came here to free my thoughts," she said softly, kicking her pretty feet back and forth. "So, can we talk? It's been two days and I miss you."

"The pool closes in like seven minutes. Say what you have to say, so we can get on with our night," I ordered, watching her closely.

Seeing that I wasn't backing down from my tough guy act, she began to talk, "Anthony is my ex-fiancé, the one I was telling you about. We ran into each other the day of the ball and he was telling me how he wanted to get back together. He said he was going to invite me to some speech he had, but I didn't pay any mind."

She looked me in the eye, continuing, "After telling him off...and spraying him with pepper spray," she giggled, "I headed home and that was when you called. I had no idea he worked for the mayor or that he was going to be at the ball. I definitely didn't know he was going to kiss me and do all that for the cameras. It looked bad, and I realize that, but I never meant to hurt you. I never wanted that to happen."

I listened to her explain the situation and knew she was being honest. Throughout the years of counseling people in my previous ministry, and even training myself to be deceiving, I could pick up the signs of a liar fairly well. Besides Marisha, of course, I had been pretty good over the years at deciphering if someone was telling the truth or not. Unable to contain my relief that Alani was not playing games, I swam back over and stood in the center of the water. She looked hopeful as she waited for me to speak.

"I can't even say I blame him."

"What do you mean?"

"Girl, you turned all kinds of heads the other night from the top politicians in the city to the waiting staff of the coliseum. You were stunning as I told you time and time again. So, I can't blame him for trying to get back what he lost."

Her cheeks became flushed even in the darkened night. She dropped her head shyly. "So, you believe me?"

"I do." I nodded and held my arms out to her. "I'm sorry that I didn't give you the chance to explain that night and I'm sorry for not answering your calls or your text messages. I'm sorry for looking at you through the window with the girls that night you came over too. That rain probably ruined your dress, huh?"

"Thank God for dryers," she said playfully, igniting a laugh between us. "What are you doing?"

"Waiting on you to jump in, so I can make up for lost time."

"I don't know how to swim," she explained with a bit of shame in her voice. She looked so cute the way she studied the water and then looked at me with fear in her eyes.

"The water isn't that deep. You could probably stand up in it. Plus, I'm here. I got you," I promised her. "Come here."

"No."

"So, you trust me with your heart, but not with your body?"

"I trust you, but…"

"But nothing. If you trust me, then bring your fine tail over here," I commanded, still opening my arms towards her and floating back and forth. "I want to kiss you under the stars, baby."

Alani sighed deeply and weighed out her options. She favored a child in that moment as she bit the inside of her lip and then surrendered all. With a hilarious flop into the water, and completely missing my open arms, she sank briefly to the bottom. I scooped her up quickly, as she flailed her arms wildly, only to realize that she could stand up straight on her own. I calmed her down with a slight laugh and two kisses to her forehead, and then brushed the wet pieces of hair that clung to her face.

"Stand up."

She did as told, but still gripped my shoulders with all her might. She trembled slightly.

"You're okay, Alani. I told you…I got you."

"I know, but it's so dark." She looked at me

and the corners of her mouth eventually moved up into a smirk. "You must think I'm so dramatic."

"Nah, I just think you're the world's most beautiful woman." I rained kisses down the side of her face, against her neck, and across her nose and cheeks. With a moan of triumph, I finally kissed her lips and backed her into the wall of the pool.

"Hey, look at me," I whispered.

She did as told.

"I also wanted to share with you the good news the other night. Guess what?"

Alani ran her hand over my wet hair and down the side of my head, nestling it against my cheek. "I'm terrible at guessing, so just tell me."

I chuckled, leaning to kiss her cheek. "Right. Well, I've been invited to speak at church for our Thanksgiving week service. I've been asked to preach a 25-minute message on Psalm 107."

"What? You're getting *back* into the pulpit? Oh, my goodness!" Alani tugged me into her embrace and jumped up and down as best she could in the water. "Congratulations! That is HUGE, Jay!"

"Yeah, thank you." I smiled, my cheek moving against hers. She trembled with excitement against me. "I can't believe it, but I know it's about that time to continue doing what I've been called to do. I'm also going to be ordained as a minister-in-training, and by Christmas, my pastor said he wants me to oversee the men's department and prison ministry. I get to talk to all the brothers about my past and how I literally lost everything, and how God restored me."

Alani pulled back so I could see her face. She was still smiling brightly, and her eyes were misty. "You see me? These are tears of joy.

Everything that happened to you and tried to break you has now returned in the form of blessings and increase, and it's only up from here. I'm so proud of you."

I nodded, searching her eyes. "Thank you. That means everything to me. Life…is definitely looking up. I feel like I have almost everything I want now."

Alani cocked her head to the side. "*Almost* everything?"

"Yeah. Almost. I just need one more confirmation on something."

Alani was already nodding, understanding what I was hinting. She wrapped her arms around my neck again and hugged me firmly. "So, what are we? What is this?"

"This is love," I confirmed. "We are together…we are building a relationship…we are establishing a connection, and we're moving in God's timing. Not our own. I can see myself being with you for a lifetime but for right now, I just want you to know how much I've missed you…and those lips."

"I couldn't have said it better," Alani purred, wrapping her arms around my neck. "I love you, Jalen."

The words sounded even better rolling off of her lips.

"Alani, I am helplessly in love with you too," I confessed.

We kissed, talked, and hung out in the pool until the wee hours of the morning, thankful that no one came down to kick us out or interrupt us. It was *our* time, and wherever life took us, we were confident that God would direct our paths.

ABOUT THE AUTHOR

Olivia Shaw-Reel had written nearly 30 books before her 30th birthday. Her award-winning novels, *Soul Cry, What God Has Joined Together, and Matters of the Hart: A Tale of the Dysfunctional Hart Sisters*, have become her biggest-selling books to date.

She also hosts *The Reel Love Podcast* with her husband, Paris. Olivia lives in Milwaukee, WI.

Visit the official storefront for updates and to purchase autographed paperbacks at **osrbooks.com**.

Follow her on Instagram and Facebook at **@oliviashawreel**.

OTHER TITLES FROM THE AUTHOR

Soul Cry, Vol. 3
What God Has Joined Together, *2-Book Series*
Baptized in Her Seduction: A Church Love Affair,
2-Book Series
Lord, Save Me From Myself, Vol. 2
Meet Me at the Altar
Full Court Mess
The Only Gift
Andrue & Sy'mone: An Urban Love Affair, *3-Book
Series*
Can't Leave Him Alone After the Love We Made,
Book 1
Kiss Me @ Midnight
Stuck Wit'chu
Sins of a Mafia Princess
Matters of the Hart: A Tale of the Dysfunctional
Hart Sisters, *3-Book Series*
In Love With Everything You Could Be
Stalked by My Pastor, *Book 1*
A Christmas Miracle
Who's Loving You This Christmas?
Saved, Sanctified, & Filled With Anxiety
Compilation

www.ingramcontent.com/pod-product-compliance
Lightning Source LLC
Chambersburg PA
CBHW050358030726
47503CB00006B/1909